More praise for *The Hole*

"A staggeringly good novel."

—*Jersey Evening Post*

"Compelling . . . Genuinely shocking."

—MARK MORRIS

"The suspense and claustrophobia become almost unbearable . . . A remarkable debut by any standards."

—*Irish Independent*

"Recommended . . . A one-sitting read . . . Perfect for escapist reading lists."

—*Library Journal*

By Guy Burt

The Hole
Sophie
The Dandelion Clock

THE HOLE

Guy Burt

BALLANTINE BOOKS
NEW YORK

A Ballantine Book
Published by The Ballantine Publishing Group

Copyright © 1993 by Guy Burt

www.ballantinebooks.com

Library of Congress Control Number: 2002090428

ISBN 0-345-44655-0

Manufactured in the United States of America

Cover design by Dreu Pennington-McNeil
Cover illustration by Phil Hefferman

First Ballantine Books Hardcover Edition: October 2001
First Ballantine Books Trade Paperback Edition: June 2002

10 9 8 7 6 5 4 3 2

For
I.M.B.
and
R.A.L.

Dear Eliot—

I thought you might find this interesting! I shall be in London from the fourteenth, if you have anything you'd like to add or discuss. Look forward to seeing you soon.

Yours, P. H.

ONE

In the last Easter term, before the Hole, life was bright and good at Our Glorious School. Charged with the fresh self-confidence that steps in on the brink of adulthood, we all knew our futures as we walked out our lives under the arches and below the walls.

The story begins, though, a little later than that; and perhaps it is still not finished. At least, I have not yet felt in me that the Hole is finished. But telling this story will, I hope, move me a step further away from it, and maybe help me to forget some of what happened.

It was a clear, unseasonably warm day when the six figures made their way across the sun-washed flags of the quad to the side of the English block. Down there, in the dark hollow of a buttress, a rusted iron stairway circled its way into the ground. One after another, they followed its spiral and disappeared into the triangular shadow. A long time passed, and the sun shifted in the sky and slipped its light through different classroom windows, briefly illuminating battered leather briefcases and untidy stacks of paper. The accumulated and forgotten detritus of the spent term grew warm for a while, and then a thin cloud began to draw over from the east and the classrooms were dulled. A single figure appeared at the head of the iron staircase and paused, looking carefully around the deserted driveways and empty cricket pitches. With hands hooked into the pockets of his clean gray trousers, he set off towards the woods that flanked the pavilion, fair hair flapping gently in the growing breeze.

And although it was not yet apparent, this figure—dwindling towards the late spring green of the woods—was now, from one viewpoint, a murderer.

"It's not even as though anyone would mind," Alex said, and went off to the small lavatory set back around the corner, taking her large and shabby knapsack with her. There was another small room there, which had most likely served once as a storage closet. Mike couldn't guess when this place had last been used for anything. The smell of it was dry and cool. There was dust between the stones of the floor that had set, become fossilized.

Mike doubled his sleeping bag up behind his back as a sort of cushion. The Hole was blank and harsh in the naked light of the bulb, like a badly adjusted TV picture. Frankie was searching through her bags for something, pulling out articles of clothing and other junk, stuffing them back in again, working seemingly at random. There was a faint, glassy sound of water into water, and then the hiss and roar of the huge gray cistern. Frankie triumphantly flourished an octagonal cardboard box.

"Anyone want some?" she asked happily. The others looked at her.

"What is it?" Geoff asked suspiciously.

"Turkish delight," returned Frankie. "Lovely. I got two boxes, just in case."

"No thanks," Mike said. He wondered idly what the second box might be in case of.

"Me neither, if it's all the same to you," Geoff said. "That stuff—it tastes like . . . I don't know, it tastes . . ."

"It's rose-flavored," Frankie said.

"No, it tastes like . . ."

Alex returned, shaking her hands violently at the wrists.

"Ah, for heaven's sake!" shouted Frankie, and a small plume of white sugar powder leapt up from the box she was holding. "You got water all *over* me."

"Did anyone think to bring a towel?" Alex asked. Mike shook his head. It hadn't crossed his mind.

"I have," said Liz. That followed, Mike decided. You'd never expect someone like Frankie to remember towels, but Liz would. He wasn't sure why he had this impression of her; it just seemed natural.

"Thanks," said Alex. "That water's too cold for me."

"What time is it now?" asked Frankie.

"Nine. Why do you need to know?" Geoff said. "You keep on asking me what bloody time it is."

"I'm tired. And I forgot my watch," Frankie said.

"How can you be tired?" Alex asked. "All we've done since four o'clock is sit around chatting."

"I haven't," Mike said. "I joined a rather fascinating little trip to see some rock formations and then hiked across the moors for an hour or two." They laughed.

"That's exactly the sort of thing Morris and friends would get up to," Geoff said.

"Thank God we *didn't* go," Alex said, with a shiver. "Last field trip was a nightmare. I spent the whole week soaking wet and half-blinded by rain." She pushed her hair back from her face and continued. "And I hate mountains. I'm not a mountain person. More a living-room person, I think."

"You can thank Martyn for it all," Frankie said.

"Yeah," Mike said. "Out of the field trip and into the Hole, to coin a phrase."

"I quite like it down here," Alex said. "I know it's not exactly comfortable—or big, for that matter—but you get the impression that, with a little care, it could be almost cozy. Some curtains, and tasteful rugs. You know."

"Funny," Frankie said. "Very funny. Ha ha."

By now, Mike thought, the field trip probably would have been across a mountain or two. He'd been on the previous expeditions, and had really rather enjoyed himself. But, of course, the chance to become involved with one of Martyn's schemes was worth any sacrifice. Which was why, he reflected wryly, he was stuck in a cellar under the English block instead of above the snowline in the Peak District. Around him the others had arranged their possessions on the floor of the cellar. Geoff, lounging on one elbow next to him, waved a hand vaguely over his knapsack and the untidy pile of clothing and tins of food that was spread next to it.

"What I still don't get is how this place could just be here, but never be used," he said. "It would make a great common room, or music room, or something."

"Half Our Glorious School isn't used," Frankie said dismissively. "My dad says the whole place needs a bloody good change of management."

"Then your dad has the full support of the entire student body," Geoff said.

"Frankie's right," Alex said. "There are places like this all over the school. That bit behind the physics department, for example. What's it used for? Nobody ever goes in there."

"That's the butterfly collection," Liz said unexpectedly. Mike always felt a lift of mild surprise when Liz spoke. "They only open it every five years or so."

"You're joking," Geoff said, staring at her. "Butterflies?"

"Typical," said Frankie with a snort. "Betcha it's some bequest or other. People are always bequesting things to us."

"Bequeathing," Mike said.

"Whatever."

"I hereby bequeath to Our Glorious School my entire collection of compromising photographs of the teaching staff, to be left on permanent display in the dining rooms," Mike said.

"I'm hungry," Alex said. She took off her round wire-rimmed glasses and started to polish them with a hanky. "How about a nearly bedtime snack?"

"Let's see what we have," Frankie said at once.

Mike grinned. "Calm down, ladies," he said. "One at a time."

"Condescending bastard," Frankie said. "This says French toast. I think I'll eat that."

"French toast?" Geoff said. "Sounds rather rude. 'Ello, dar-lin', how about some French toast, then?"

Mike shuffled lower on his sleeping bag and closed his eyes against the hard light of the bulb. "I thought French toast was when you stuck your tongue out and licked the butter off," he said. Alex snorted with laughter, and then stopped herself rather guiltily.

"Disgusting, Mikey," Frankie said.

"Not as disgusting as that Turkish stuff," Geoff said. "It tastes so bloody *pink*, that's all."

This is how it all began. But remember, we were very young then.

I can hear Martyn saying to us, before we went down there, "This is an experiment with real life." That was what he called it.

"Isn't that a bit ambitious?" I asked, and he smiled.

Martyn's smile was wide and easy, and it sat happily in Mar-tyn's round fair face. Teachers knew what Martyn was. He was a thoughtful, rather slow boy who could be trusted with responsibility. He was always friendly, always willing to chat with old Mr. Stevens about fishing or stop by to take a look at Dr. James's garden. He was a good boy; sensible. Stanford once said, "That boy is a damned fine head of library," which I think probably surprised the staff as much as the pupils—Stanford not being known for tender words about anyone.

We also knew who Martyn was, and revelled in the complete and wonderful illusion he had created. Because we knew that it was Martyn who was behind the Gibbon incident; Martyn who orchestrated the collapse of the End of Term Address; Martyn who was perhaps the greatest rebel Our Glorious School had ever seen. The duplicity of Martyn's life was, in our eyes, something admirable and enviable. Perhaps if we had taken the time to examine this, we might have been closer to guessing what was later to happen. But it never occurred to us that the deception might involve more than the two layers we saw.

Strange how time changes things around us.

Strange how we change with time.

Sadly, schools deal in the sale and exchange of knowledge, not wisdom. And it was wisdom that we could have used back then, all that time ago. And we were not equipped. We were not ready.

"Isn't that a bit ambitious?" I said, and the voice was a child's voice, trusting and entirely innocent. And the voice that answered it was old; far too old for the round, smiling face and pale blue eyes.

"Oh, I don't think so," Martyn said to me.

"My uncle likes this stuff, I think," Frankie said, staring at her drink. "Weird man, my uncle. Very famous, of course."

"Famous for what?" Alex asked, rolling over on her sleeping bag.

"Being weird." Frankie giggled. "Let's have some more in here, Geoff." She held out her mug and Geoff, unscrewing the cap of the whisky bottle, poured her another. "Seriously. He does stuff for TV."

"I can see gunge stuck to your teeth," Geoff said. Frankie grinned and wiped a cuff across her mouth.

"Sick," Mike said dispassionately. "I wish Martyn could have found more civilized companions for me."

"Now I've got fluff," Frankie complained.

It was really just three of them; Alex had rolled over again and was staring at the ceiling, twisting a fold of her shirt through her fingers, while Liz had her head in her notebook, holding it too close and chewing the end of a black pen. The tip of one of her ears, Mike noticed, was poking up through her hair, pale against the brown. She kept brushing the hair out of her eyes. Mike wondered if she'd ever thought of tying it back or something. As he watched, she glanced up at him, and then flicked her gaze back to the notebook, scribbling.

A pleasant calm came over the Hole that evening; that first evening, when everyone was still pretty much their own self. Geoff and Frankie offered the bottle of whisky around, and Mike had a little. They talked about the past term, and what they were going to do, and laughed about the imagined exploits and discomforts of the field trip.

"When are you guys going to quit the party and settle down?" Alex asked, looking up. "It's nearly midnight, and I'm exhausted."

"It's eleven fifty; do you know where your children are?" Liz said.

Frankie crossed her legs. "C'mon, Alex, it's only just starting," she said. "Why didn't anyone bring a stereo?"

"Because we don't want to be stuck with your taste in music," Geoff told her.

Mike settled back on his knapsack. "I can't say I do know where my children are," he said. "Last time I saw them they were heading for some poky old school with this fair-haired guy. Haven't seen them since."

"You don't think he shut them in a cellar and left them there, do you?" Geoff said.

"I declare that might be the case," Mike agreed, nodding owlishly.

"When we get out," Frankie said, "isn't everyone going to know that we weren't on the field trip?"

"Of course they are," Geoff said wearily. "But that doesn't matter, does it? The school thinks we're at home, our parents think we're up north somewhere. And there's no reason why either should ever be disillusioned."

"Oh, yeah," Frankie said.

"We have been through all this before," Geoff pointed out.

Mike rested his head on one of the more padded parts of his knapsack and laced his fingers over his chest.

"One good thing about Our Glorious School," he said, "is that we do stick together."

"We'll probably go down as a legend," Frankie said. "Everything Martyn does is legendary." She hiccupped loudly. " 'Scuse me. The shock of becoming a legend has given me hiccups."

"I've done my teeth," Mike said, "if anyone else wants to use the hovel."

I put down the stack of paper and sat back, stretching my legs and looking out of the half-open attic window over the trees outside. There was warm air drifting across the room, and dust hesitated in the blades of sunlight that portioned the table and floor. Downstairs, the sound of the front door opening and my mother's voice. I pushed back the chair and settled things the way I like to find them, jam-jars of pencils and pens, books and scraps and jottings, an old bottle of ink smelling like the insides of school desks. There were footsteps on the stairs as I closed the window against the eventual night breezes, and the door opened.

"Hi," I said. "Come in."

"So this is where it's all going on," he said.

"This is where it's all going to go on," I corrected. "So far I've only just started; and there's a lot to write."

"Don't I know it," he said. "You can see the school from here. I didn't realize."

"You've never been up here," I reminded him.

"You never invited me."

"Well, it was a dump until a few weeks ago. I had to clear it all out; junk and dust and old carpets and other shit. And then I had to get a sofa up here, and the bookcases, and the table. Took a while."

"I'm impressed. Was it worth it?"

I sighed. "I don't know. Yes, I think. It's easier to concentrate on it all when you're up here; when you can see the school and when there's nothing else to distract you. I've got quite a lot done—there's this lot of notes, and other stuff."

"I love you very much," he said quietly. "And I think you're very brave."

I laughed nervously. "Yeah, well. Someone's got to do it, right?"

"Right."

"And I love you, too."

"As if I didn't know. I don't think we do good dialogue, Liz."

"Then I won't write it down," I promised.

• • •

They talked for a while, trying to get comfortable on the hard floor of the cellar. Then Frankie went off and sorted herself out in the bathroom, the two other girls changed in the seclusion of the little room facing the lavatory, and eventually they switched out the light and settled down for their first night.

Mike lay awake and turned over in his mind the events of the afternoon and evening, looking at them as much as possible from an outsider's point of view. He'd left home that afternoon to meet up with the Peak District expedition minibus, which had already gone; and, when the others had arrived, they had made their way to the steps by the English department, forgotten and rusted almost to pieces. At the foot of the stairway was a small square piece of open ground, littered with beer cans and thick with rubbish and the skeletal holly leaves of many years past. Twisted pieces of iron railwork jutted painfully from the tangle of cigarette packs and bits of rotting newspaper. They stepped cautiously into a short passage, the bright March sunlight curtaining the darkness for a moment as they hesitated. The door to the Hole was on their right, a wooden door with dark brown paint that had cracked in long sharp lines. The hasp and padlock were dull, zinc-colored. Martyn had produced a key from his trouser pocket; his trousers were neatly pressed, Mike had noticed with a smile. Martyn was always precise with things like that.

When the door was opened, Mike had wondered who had been the last person to breathe the air of the room. Martyn had a rope ladder, and they climbed down. There were no stairs in the Hole, not any longer.

The thought came to him, then, as he lay looking back on the day, that the Hole was not just forgotten, but had never been remembered at all; that it had been built and left empty for Martyn and them. He smiled, and told himself that he no more believed in Fate than he did in God.

Ignoring his own heartbeat, he could just detect the slow breathing of the others in the Hole, bathing in sleep. Mike, under a firmament with no stars, turned on his side and sank to join them.

Two

The first full day dawned in darkness, to the muted clamor of Geoff's alarm clock. The transition from the soft darkness to the light of the bulb was caustic.

"When I'm feelin' blue," Alex sang in the lavatory. "Yah-ta da da *da*." Liz had the frying pan out and was cracking eggs into the holes she'd torn in the fried bread. The Hole began to fill with the strong aroma of hot lard and cooking.

"Quite the housewife," Frankie said, half-admiringly. "Everything I cook goes flat and gray."

"Get your hair out the way," Geoff said. "I don't need a high-fiber breakfast."

"Hm? Oh." Liz tucked her hair into the neck of her shirt.

They ate; Mike discovered that he was hungry. Geoff found an apple and broke it in half.

"That was delicious," Mike said. "What's next?"

"The walking appetite prepares to avenge his incarceration

by eating his fellows," Alex said. "No—it's too horrible to watch. There they go; one after the other. Like gingerbread men."

"Thanks, Alex, how kind."

"Think nothing of it. I'm sure you'd do the same."

"Look out, folks. She's dangerous this morning," Geoff said. "Nothing like Alex before midday."

"You know what I want?" Alex said.

"A muzzle?" Geoff said sweetly.

"Very funny. A chair. I'd give—well, a lot, just to get a nice chair down here."

"Very homely," Geoff said. "You always sound like some-one's mother."

"Why didn't you bring one?" Liz asked.

"Never thought of it. I never thought I'd miss them that much, actually. But after you've got up in the morning, you sit on a chair, yes? And I haven't got one. I feel distressed."

"I feel distressed, too," Geoff said cryptically. "And it has nothing to do with chairs."

"OK," Mike said. "I want a bath. A large cast-iron bath with claws on the feet and huge brass taps. And I want a lot of hot water to go in it."

"I didn't know men were allowed to do that," Alex said. Mike grinned wearily.

"What, wash?"

"Right."

"Good one."

Alex wrinkled her nose. "Three days without a bath. Yeugh."

"I like baths," Geoff said. "But I can go without."

"Sure. But are we really expected to put up with it?" Alex

smiled. "That's going to be the really hard part, you know. I'm going to miss all the nice things from home." She thought briefly. "Like clean companions."

"Frankie's quiet this morning," observed Geoff.

"Frankie's exhausted this morning," Frankie retorted. "Frankie could have done with another four hours' sleep. But no; Frankie has to do what everybody else wants, and put up with being criticized for not talking."

"Sunny days are here again," Mike said.

Liz wandered off with the dirty frying pan to the lavatory, where a single cold-water tap dripped into a grating on the floor. They heard the loud splashing of water as she rinsed the pan. On the floor of the Hole, the camping-gas stove fizzed quietly. Frankie stared at it suspiciously.

"I knew someone who had one of those things under his bed, and it exploded," she said. "It knocked all the glass out of his window and ruined everything."

"Did he die?" Geoff asked with interest.

"He wasn't in the room at the time."

"Oh."

"Did anyone bring any dish soap?" Liz called.

"No," Mike shouted back. "There's a bar of soap on the pipe just inside the door."

"You mean I ate off plates washed like that?" Frankie said. "That's vile! I could catch something horrible. Some disease or something. This place hasn't been cleaned in ages."

"Neither have I," Geoff said cheerfully.

"You're just saying that to make me sick," Frankie told him.

"Besides," said Mike, "even if you did catch something, it

probably wouldn't want you." Frankie threw the empty Turkish delight box at him and it spiralled erratically through the air, sifting thin sheets of white dust on its way.

"If Frankie's going to piss around, shouldn't we shut that thing off?" Geoff suggested, pointing to the stove. "Don't you think they look like spaceships from low-budget fifties sci-fi movies? Just turn it upside down and spray it silver and you have an instant interstellar craft."

Alex turned down the hard blue flames until they sank into silence and vanished. Liz came through with the clean frying pan and Mike, who could smell the trace of unburnt gas in the still air of the Hole, remembered a time when he himself had taken a gas stove out on to the back lawn of his house to change the cylinder; and, because the old cylinder was not quite spent, a thin cold fluid had tumbled out of the puncture in its top and vaporized. The grass stems shimmered momentarily as it melted away. He smiled at himself; that must have been—all of ten years ago. Perhaps longer.

"I think I'd like a pillow," Geoff said.

I remember sitting on the bed of Martyn's study, summer sunlight on the wall and some old seventies music playing quietly in the background. Eight of us there; Vernon stroking the leaves of one of the many plants that were positioned at regular intervals around the room; Geoff reading the cover notes on some of Martyn's albums; Martyn himself, glass of red wine in one hand, smiling and talking about the end of term.

"I simply find it a little ... insulting that the school expects me to be interested in that sort of thing. I think the Head feels the same way. Have you noticed the way he keeps everything to a minimum?"

"Yeah, the guy wants to go home as much as anyone," Steve muttered.

"But our dear Deputy Head—that's where I do take exception."

"Law is an ass," Vernon said, looking over. "As someone once nearly said."

"Law is a *pompous* ass who imposes his pomposity on everyone in earshot," Martyn corrected. "I think it is about time that old Law was forced to look on the funny side for once."

"Law wouldn't see the funny side of a circular joke," Lisa said.

"Maybe so, maybe so. But—as the Head so often takes the trouble to remind us—one cannot help but fail if one does not *try*."

"And what true words those are," murmured Vernon reverently. "Could I have some more wine? Thanks."

"This," Martyn said, holding up his glass, "is Hungarian. And while it may not be as subtle as we have recently got used to—don't laugh, Steve—it is undeniably cheap; and I have rather a lot of it."

"Where did it come from?" Lisa asked.

"Now, now—you know the rules."

"OK. But how cheap, exactly?"

Vernon stopped stroking the plant and straightened up. "Probably free, I should think. If you know where to look."

"Gibbon's in the quad," Geoff said. "Stupid twat's looking very angry."

"He's still pissed off about his car," Lisa said.

"Gibbon," Martyn said quietly. "And there's someone else who needs to be—to lighten up a bit."

With the normal trivialities that conspire to fill a day removed, time spent in the Hole began to slide away from the normal stanchions that pinion our lives; hours, mornings and afternoons, breaks in conversation, became fluid things that changed and re-shaped themselves around the occupants. Mike found himself watching the others far more closely than he ever had before. That first morning, he remained quieter than usual; learning more about the people he could see than he had realized was possible. He could tell their breathing apart; he saw the way that they sat—Alex neatly, legs crossed; Frankie, as often as not, curled on one side. Liz, staying quiet, occasionally leafed through a small notebook.

Some things that he began to notice were irksome. At other times, he spotted little patterns of behavior that pleased him strangely. The door, high in the wall above Alex's head, was al-ways at the upward edge of his vision.

"The way I see it," Frankie was saying, "it doesn't make much difference whether you lie on purpose or just make a mis-take. The result's the same either way."

Alex frowned. "No it's not. I mean, if I told a lie, then I've done something wrong. But if I just make a mistake, then it's no one's fault."

"I know the difference," Geoff said brightly. "If you lie to someone and they find out, you're in shit. But if you just made a mistake, they don't mind."

"Yes they do," said Frankie.

Geoff gave it some thought. "Yeah," he agreed. "They do sometimes, I suppose."

"What about white lies?" Mike put in. Alex pulled her little wire-rimmed glasses down her nose.

"I don't know," she said.

"Same as anything else," Frankie said. "It doesn't matter whether you lie or not, it's what you say that counts."

Liz looked up. "There is a difference," she said.

"I told a lie once," Geoff began, but Alex interrupted him.

"Hang on, Geoff. I want to hear what Liz is saying."

"I just said there's a difference," said Liz, mildly surprised.

"Which is?"

"The effect that what you say has on you, I think. Frankie's right; it doesn't alter the meaning of the words if you say them as a mistake or if you lie deliberately. But you're right, too, because telling a lie has to be something you choose to do, and that choice affects who you are."

Again, Mike realized that he was finding things out about his companions.

"Nah," Geoff said. "Not much affects who I am."

"Maybe you don't notice," Liz said.

"Oh, don't be patronizing."

"Well, there you have it," Mike said. "Arguments settled, conflicts resolved, both viewpoints guaranteed to be represented." A look of annoyance passed briefly across Liz's face, and he immediately regretted the flippant comment.

"Bloody pink-flavored stuff," Frankie proclaimed, pulling out her box of Turkish delight. "Anyone? OK, I'll eat it myself."

"I told a lie once," said Geoff. "I never got into trouble for it, though. I got into trouble for telling a lie I didn't tell, instead."

"Do we want to hear this one, folks?" Frankie asked. "Aw, shit. Go on then, Geoff."

"I told my teacher I'd lied to her about spilling ink. I was only eight."

Mike thought. "So what was the lie you didn't get into trouble for?"

"That was it. You see, I hadn't lied about spilling the ink. Someone else had done it. I lied about lying about it."

"Why did you do it?"

"What, spill the ink? I just told you, I didn't. That was—"

"No, not that. Why did you lie?"

"Oh." Geoff shrugged. "To find out. Besides, she was a teacher. I thought she'd know."

"Why didn't you tell her you'd lied about lying?"

Geoff grinned crazily. "You think she'd have believed me? Ha!"

"That was hardly worth it," Alex said, trying to force the smile out of her face. "Your bloody stories."

"Ha! Every time!"

"Can we talk about something else?" Frankie asked, pleadingly.

"Sex," said Geoff.

"If I had two chairs, I could put them facing one another and sleep on them. They're wonderful items of furniture." Alex sighed. "I like ones with wide arms you can balance drinks on."

Yesterday, I took a walk by the river, and in the end found myself going through old friendships in my mind. And old friends, too; not much of that sort of thing survived the Hole. I think that many people end up strangers to themselves. Your mental image of other people is simplified and incomplete, and most of us realize this. What we maybe don't realize is that we have the same kind of picture of ourselves. One day you turn around, prompted perhaps by something you've said or done that doesn't feel quite right; and the person you find you are is someone new to you, someone whom you don't know at all.

I once knew a man who killed himself. In a manner of speaking. He changed his name, moved to a new house, got a new job and a new life with a new family in some bright young town away from where he'd once been. There was nothing left of him. At least if you keep the engine running in a closed garage, or step off a cliff, there is some physical part of you that remains, a dignified loss. I don't think I ever forgave him for that.

As I sat by the river with this moving through my mind, and the summer air languid on my back and shoulders, two girls walked past with a dog on a leash.

"Hi," one of them called.

I waved back. "Enjoy your walk."

They laughed. "We will!" one of them shouted, and they took the side path down through the woods.

I found a stone and threw it far out over the water, wondered what it disturbed as it fell. Then I made my way back home.

Beside my closet is a cardboard box full of things waiting to be taken up to the attic. In there are more fragments of a story whose limits I still don't know; the story of Martyn, and who he was. On top of the papers and notebooks, school reports and exam papers and other related material I'd gathered over the time since I'd known him, were two small piles of BASF cassettes and a portable tape recorder.

Somewhere in there was the real truth, the absolute story (if there can be such a thing). And more than anything else, I did not want to listen to those cassettes. It had been a long time, since they were recorded, since the words were imprinted on oxide. The story in there is not my story, but it impinges on my story; and it is the only thing I have to show that the Hole was not an elaborate fantasy, a game gone wrong, something accidental. Because it was none of those things. I was there.

All of which is to follow, soon. Childhood is the formation of the adult that we become. Once the basic structure is defined, you live it out according to the rules that have been set within yourself. Adulthood is understanding those rules and building on those foundations. Quite where and how the change from one state to the other happens is variable. Some people never really become adults, never really know who they are. They lose half their life that way, thinking that they are gaining; they don't know where to look for the materials with which to build their life, when all the time they should be looking to themselves.

Three

Mike had to step over the splashed puddles from the lunchtime washing-up to reach the lavatory. The small room was cold, and the forty-watt bulb overhead glowed dismally. There was a steady dripping as the greasy water wound its way over the rim of the grating in the floor and fell away, down into some huge underground channel carrying the fragmentary residues of millions of lives away into the sea. He smiled uncertainly at the image and zipped his trousers, turned and stepped back to join the others in the brighter light around the corner.

"Siesta time," Frankie said, stretching. "It's quite inhuman to do anything except sleep after a meal."

"Great philosophy," muttered Geoff.

"I thought siestas were a sort of car," Alex said brightly.

"Please, not that again," Mike begged her. "Let's try and give it a rest for just three days."

"Less than that," Alex said. "Two and a half days."

"This evening, I think we should have a housebreaking party," Geoff said. "To settle us in properly."

"Don't you mean a housewarming party?"

"That," he said, "depends entirely on who you invite."

"The noonday bulb sears the land," Mike said. "Cicadas and—other creepy crawlies—sing merrily in the orange groves."

"Do you think inviting Mike is a good idea?" Alex said seriously.

"Hm. Probably a very bad idea, actually. But it would be cruel to leave him out, so he'll have to come."

"Frankie's got to come, too," Frankie said. "After she's had her siesta."

"A lone peasant woman toils across the turf with her bundle," Mike continued. "But—wait! It's Frankie, carrying a linen-wrapped parcel of Turkish delight to sell for pennies at the distant market."

"Shut up," Alex said.

"I wish we hadn't had those bread things with seeds on," Frankie complained. "I've got bits stuck in my teeth."

Liz looked up and grinned at Mike.

"What?" he said.

"Nothing."

"What is it?"

"Let us see what we have in the secret supply," Geoff said, unbuckling his knapsack. "Oh dear."

"What?" Frankie said.

"All my Ribena has turned into funny-shaped bottles," Geoff said, sounding outraged. "Look! What does this mean? Gin . . . whisky . . . some other stuff that's not readily identifiable . . . some tin cups . . . this is disgraceful! Obviously someone has switched knapsacks with me."

"Ah, well," Frankie said. "We'll just have to drink it instead."

"I guess so," Geoff agreed.

"Not now, surely?" Mike said. "It's only just gone three o'clock."

"No. This evening, you daft dork. Instead of watching TV or engaging in illegal practices with animals or whatever you normally do."

"That's crass," Alex said.

"Cress?" Mike said. "Talking of practices with animals and cress, remember the End of Term Address?"

Frankie snorted abruptly with laughter. "That was the funniest thing in the world," she proclaimed, when she'd stopped giggling. "I nearly wet myself."

"So did most of the school," Geoff agreed.

"Not a dry seat in the house," Liz said, smiling.

"The look on Law's face," Geoff began, and then laughed aloud. "Shit, that's one to tell the grandchildren."

"It was entirely his own fault," Frankie said.

Alex scratched her nose. "No it wasn't. All the poor sod did was live next door to a farm and annoy Martyn."

"It's enough, it's enough," Mike said. "People have suffered for less."

"They certainly have," Liz agreed.

We lay with the evening sunlight on the wall, with the sheets drawn half across us, with the trees turning the color of hot metal outside the window.

"I wish," I said.

"What do you wish?"

I smiled. "Many things."

"Right now, what do you wish?"

"Oh . . . that the summer could go on forever. It's like something lifted out of a dream, this summer."

"It is?"

I squeezed his shoulder. "Don't. Of course it is."

"If you say so."

"I'm the writer. If I say it's a summer out of a dream, then it bloody well is one."

He laughed. "Do you know something?"

"Tell me."

"You're a romantic."

"I am not!"

"Yes you are. You pretend that you're not, but you are."

"Maybe. So. What do you wish?"

"My wish is a secret."

"It can't be," I said. "Tell me."

He thought for a while. "It's a true wish."

"Yes?"

"I promise to tell you when you've finished—the writing. OK?"

"OK. Why?"

"Because I want it to come after all that."

I wasn't really listening. "That's nice."

"Yes. . . ."

We lay and dreamed together for a long time, until the clock showed seven.

"Liz?"

"Hm?"

"We can't stay here all night."

"Why not?"

"We can't."

"I'd like to," I said.

"So would I. But that doesn't make much difference."

"Just a little while longer, then," I said.

Separate lives are fine, of their sort; but shared life is something completely new and distinct. Even if the sharing is only for short times. That evening, despite our closeness—or perhaps because of it—the Hole seemed very far off, something half-recalled at the end of sleep. The world around me had been reduced to an encapsulation of a few hours; everything outside that was dim and fogged. If we could live all our lives in the present, with no recourse to what has gone before or what might yet be, we would be so much the simpler for it. But in fact the here and now of life is all too often the least considered, while thoughts of the past and expectations of the future conspire to tangle our minds with irreconcilable regrets and hopes. That is part of what makes us the people we are, I suppose; but it was very good, for a little time, to ignore the outside and simply be together.

And eventually we dressed, and made off into our individual evenings, where different things would be demanded of us.

"And when he got back, he'd missed two years and a whole set of public exams. Screwed his whole life up." Frankie paused. "Tough shit, I suppose, but nobody really liked him anyway."

"I didn't even know the guy," Mike said.

By the time shown on their watches, the afternoon had begun to become evening. Liz was taking packets of rice and cardboard cartons out of her knapsack and arranging them around her in preparation for supper.

"This isn't quite what I expected, you know," Geoff said.

"What?"

"This. The Hole. I mean, with Martyn you normally expect something more—I don't know. . . ."

"A bit more bang for your buck?" Frankie suggested.

"Yeah. More flashy. You know his track record, the practical jokes and so on."

"Practical jokes writ large," Mike said. "Gibbon. And the Law thing."

"He did say that this was an experiment with real life," Alex said. "Maybe it's different."

"You mean Martyn might have got mature in his old age?" Geoff said. "I rather doubt that."

Mike thought it over. It had never struck him that Martyn's previous escapades were immature: in fact, he sometimes wondered just how much of the bite behind them was perceived by most of the school. Most people saw Martyn's constructions as elaborate pranks. But if that was all they were, why had Gibbon left so abruptly? Mike shook his head. No, Martyn was mature enough, all right. Part of the fun of watching him was to see how inventively the next incident would be concealed.

And there was something else, too. Teachers might be strange, but they weren't all stupid; and someone who could so consistently cover his tracks and maintain his status with the staff was far from a simple prankster.

"What does that mean, anyway?" Frankie was saying. "An experiment with real life. Sounds a bit bloody pretentious to me."

"Most things do, to you," Geoff said.

"Screw you," she smiled primly. "So?"

"I suppose it means that it's—well, more serious than the other stuff," Alex said.

"Some of the other stuff was pretty serious, too," Geoff replied. "That's what was so funny about it. I mean, it's one thing to suggest quietly that the Deputy Head buggers sheep once in a while—"

"I bet he does," Frankie put in.

"But it's something else again to do what—what he did," Geoff finished, grinning hugely. "God, what kind of person thinks up things like that?"

"Persons like Martyn," Frankie said. "Weird bloke. Not as weird as my uncle, but getting on that way."

"Hands up who wants to eat," Mike said. "I'm hungry."

"It's disgusting that you eat so much and stay so thin," Frankie said. "You make me sick."

"You know what makes me sick?" Geoff asked.

"What?"

"Sticking two fingers down my throat," he told her smugly.

I remember sitting in the beer garden at the back of the Horseman, quite early, with only a few passing tourists and a couple of young families at the other tables. Lisa came out from the bar with drinks, and we talked a while. Not that we were friends; not even more than acquaintances, really. I had met her mostly in Martyn's study, where she was as much part of the gang as any of us. But outside that one room I hardly saw her at all, and she seemed very different as she sat, holding her glass, with the dark green of the hedge behind her. In fact, she was not how I had thought she was at all.

For one thing, she was a pretty girl; something you would think would have been noticed, and commented on, in the atmosphere of tense, rather furtive sexuality that pervaded Our Glorious School. But it seemed to me, looking back, that I'd not heard anything about Lisa from any of the boys in my year. Partly, perhaps, because she was off limits in the male catalog of available females; she was, after all, Martyn's girlfriend, and his popularity would have conferred on her a measure of personal space which a lot of girls lacked. But the main reason, I am sure, is that when I had last seen her, at school, her prettiness had not been so evident.

"Is that what you wanted?" she asked uncertainly.

"That's fine. Thanks." The beer was cool and friendly. I ran a finger down the condensation on the glass and then crossed the line I'd drawn.

"Is this OK?" she asked. "I don't want to bore you or take up your time."

"Of course it's OK. Do you want to stay here, or go to my house? It's a bit messy, but then the air isn't exactly warm today."

"I don't mind. Yes. I'd like to go somewhere else."

"Right. Just let me finish this."

I looked at her closely. She *had* got prettier. Certainly enough to put me in the shade. But there was something about her—either her manner, or the way she was sitting, which was urgent, somehow.

She stood up, and for an instant when the light caught her face I saw a shadow of something like terror, or desperation, below the surface. And I recognized it at once.

"Yes," I said, "Let's go. It's more comfortable at home."

She nodded. As we rounded the corner of the building, moving out of sight of the other people in the pub garden, she said, "I want to talk to you about Martyn."

I kept my eyes ahead. "I know." I had wondered how long it would take her.

After supper, with time pulling in so that, outside, it would soon be night, the group readied itself on the floor of the Hole for talking and drinking.

"It's in the way that you use it—tah, da," hummed Alex, holding a clear plastic beaker half-full of Chianti on her knee. "Has anyone got any chips or cheesy things?"

"I've got some tubular things in a bag," said Mike. "But they're a bit squashed and they've been open a while."

"Ah. OK, forget it."

"I'll eat 'em," Geoff offered.

"Vile," Frankie said. Mike found the chips and Geoff waved one about a bit before dunking it in his wine and eating it.

"Soggy little sods, aren't they?" he said. "Maybe we should save them till later, when no one will notice."

"They must be better than the Chianti," Alex said.

"Tastes like piss," Frankie agreed, emptying her cup. "More please, Mikey."

Mike refilled her cup.

"How do you know if it tastes like piss?" Geoff asked with interest.

"It would probably taste the same coming up as going down," Mike admitted, and sniggered. "But it was cheap. I wasn't going to lash out for you lot."

"Cheers, amigo."

"I have some, um . . ." said Liz, and, after undoing the top flap of her knapsack, produced several brown bottles.

"Liz, is that beer?" asked Mike.

"Yes."

Mike scratched one ear. "Isn't that something? You have hidden depths."

She flashed him a quick smile. "I like beer."

"You know what they say," cautioned Geoff. "Beer then wine goes down fine. Wine then beer—"

"Makes you queer," Frankie and Mike joined in.

"Too true," added Frankie with feeling.

"Anyone?" Liz asked.

"I'll join you," said Mike. The others, already holding cups of wine, refused.

With the mug of beer on the floor beside him, Mike undid his sleeping-bag zipper all the way, transforming it into a quilted poncho, which he arranged around his shoulders.

"I thought caves were supposed to be warm," he said.

Geoff considered. "Only in relation to bloody freezing," he said. "And this isn't a cave. It's a cellar. On top of which, I think the warm-cave scenario presupposes animal skins and suchlike crap."

Frankie produced a penknife. "I'm going to do a cave picture," she announced.

"Don't bother. Write who we are, though," Geoff said. "Class of the Hole."

"Original," commented Alex.

"In case anyone ever finds this place."

"Nobody ever comes here," Frankie said. "There are out-of-date and useless bits like this all over."

"If there's something out of date and completely without use, you can bet Our Glorious School will have it," Alex said.

"Julian whatsisname went into the showers near fourth arch and wasn't seen again for three years."

"Was he OK?" asked Geoff, feigning horror.

"He was bloody clean," Mike said. "But seriously, most of the teachers are out of date and totally without use. Some of them are dead, I think."

"What, and no one's noticed yet?"

"Yeah."

"That explains the good grading I got for history, at any rate," Frankie said with a grin.

"Living history," Mike said.

"What?"

"That's what Our Glorious School is. Something left over from the nineteenth century. The staff are living history, too. And so are we, by being part of it."

"Oh good, I'm part of history," Frankie said. "I like that. I'll put that in my next essay."

"Not so long to go before you can forget all about essays and so on," Geoff told her.

"Who's going to revise like good children?" Frankie asked. "Not me!"

"I've always maintained that revision assumes you learnt

something in the first place," Mike said. "It's no good me revising. I don't know anything."

"Yeah, they should call it panic learning," Alex said.

"Bullshit, Mikey," Geoff said. "You'll cram up three weeks before the exams and get your predictions." Mike shrugged.

"Pour me another," Frankie said, and the Chianti bottle with its straw wrapping did the rounds. Liz, after obvious thought, opened a second beer for herself and passed one to Mike. It was strong and metallic.

"Why do you drink beer?" Geoff asked.

"I don't think it's fair to say that we're living in the nineteenth century, just because we happen to go to school here," Alex said. "Most of the school reckon that things should be modernized. It's just the staff that get in the way."

"Are you trying to say I'm not part of living history after all?" Frankie said.

Liz looked at the brown bottle in her hand. "I told you; I like it," she said. "And it makes me think of—things, remember things. You know?"

"Distant visions of your long-past youth, you mean?" Geoff asked.

"Something like that."

"Only memories Chianti brings back to me are ones of falling over parked cars in Italy," Frankie said.

"When did you go to Italy, Frankie?" Alex asked.

"Christmas. Very nice, I must say. And very cheap booze, too."

"I wish we went abroad more often," Mike said. "We don't, though. I'd like to go to Italy."

"We've given up on holidays," Alex said. "There's no time of year when the whole family's free at once."

"Most people don't drink to remember," Geoff said. "I thought they drank to forget."

"Most people drink to get drunk," Frankie said firmly.

"I wonder if that's true," Mike said.

"Sure is."

"What about drinking because you like the taste of it?" Alex said.

"If that was true, Ribena would be the nation's favorite drink," Geoff said.

"And you wouldn't have that glass of Chianti in your hand," Frankie added triumphantly.

Alex pulled a face. "*Touché.* But there's a long stretch of road between relaxed and drunk."

"Where are you?"

She smiled. "Relaxed, Geoff. That's all."

"Relaxed is a good place to be. I wish this beer was colder," said Mike.

"I thought you were complaining about cold," Alex said.

"That was different."

To set the record straight, then: We did not know, when we went into the Hole, who Martyn was—any more than we knew who we were. But our mistakes about Martyn were to have more effect on us than any other mistakes in our lives.

That genius and madness are almost interchangeable terms has become a cliché of the psychiatric age. I think, however, that to make such an assertion is to acknowledge the presence of both attributes in the human mind. And that was something that we tried not to think about afterwards, as well.

It may even be that science has not yet coined the word that we might use to describe Martyn; which is another reason why these words, telling his story and ours, will have to do in place of one. Wherever Martyn is now, the story will go on. And while a small part of me is curious, and wants to follow that thread to its conclusion, the rational levels of my mind know only that he is gone now, and that there should be no reason to fear any longer.

FOUR

And now, I think, we have introduced ourselves comprehensively enough. We did little finding out in those three days; we talked, and drank, and became bored and grew tired of the company of the others. None of us had been forced to live in quite this way before, crammed in with people whose habits and quirks soon became tiresome and annoying. Irritation showed in a variety of ways; the sarcastic remarks, the little slights passed off for innocent comments. Nothing big. Nothing important. None of us was quite clear about what we were involved in. There were one or two qualms about the upcoming examinations, one or two regrets that we were stuck down a cellar instead of revising. Most of the time we waited from moment to moment, in a way that—in retrospect—appears obviously characteristic of childhood.

Past, present and future: all places on one line that maybe spans from a beginning to an end, maybe just continues. You get into the habit of looking at only a small portion of it—

how often do you look back at things gone and actually learn from them? How often are you taken roughly by the shoulders, wrenched about, *forced* to look into what might be? Perhaps it has already happened; perhaps it never will.

One thing that stands in the future like a wall built of stone and ashes is death; and the death of someone close to you can sometimes open up a brief avenue of sight into our own futures. Death is a strange and awful concept in the mind of man, and through his lifetime man has chosen many houses for his fear. Where do these images of dust and dry clay spring from? What compulsion is it within us that insists on robing death in familiar garments, however cold and forbidding? And why is death always to be found beneath the ground? But this is a question that is its own answer.

The story moves on. In me, the idea and recollection of the Hole is sharper now, and the faces and voices have settled into their allocated positions more exactly than I had thought they would. That night came and went in blackness, and the second day began only seven hours later, because the habits of our waking and sleeping are slow to alter.

Mike opened his eyes and saw the dark gray outline of the end of his pillow. The shadow of a dream slipped past him, and the moment he tried to think what it had been it vanished completely. Blinking, he turned and rubbed at his face and neck, squinting to try and make out the numerals on his watch; but he could not. Through the haze of sleepiness he became aware of a muted light, and he rocked himself up on one elbow to peer about him. Liz, some five feet to his left, was turned away from him, reading a book with a pocket flashlight. Mike smiled. The secret life of Liz Sheardon, he thought, and rolled onto his back. At the sound of his movement, Liz looked over her shoulder.

"Morning, sleepyhead," she whispered.

"Hi," Mike whispered back. "How long have you been awake?"

"Too long." She sat up a bit, pulling her sleeping bag up to her chin. "Did I wake you?"

"No, I think I was ready for it. I feel pretty rough, though."

Liz giggled. "I had too many beers. Did you hear me creep out for a pee at three o'clock?"

"No," Mike said, smiling.

"Lucky I had the flashlight, or I would have ended up walking on people."

"What made you bring a flashlight?"

She shrugged. "Light bulbs burn out sometimes."

"I'm impressed," Mike said. "You've really been thinking about this, haven't you?"

"In what way?"

"Like you were the only person to think of bringing a towel. And now this. No huge deal, but I hardly thought at all about what I stuffed into my bag."

"I suppose I'm just used to looking after myself."

"That's no bad thing," Mike said, wondering exactly what she meant.

"Maybe." There was a pause. "Mike?"

"Yep?"

"Did you have a dream last night?"

"Not that I remember. Why?"

"You shouted something."

Mike felt amusement and embarrassment creep over him. "I did? What like?"

"Oh, I didn't catch it. Just now. Before you woke up."

"Talking to myself already. I remember old Marmalade on last year's field trip shouting out, 'Rabbits! Oh *fuck!*' really loudly, and waking up everyone but himself."

"Yes?"

"Yeah." Mike smiled at the memory of the fuss that had ensued.

Liz was looking up at the ceiling. "With the flashlight down here, you could almost believe that there was nothing above us," she whispered. "Just nothing at all." It took Mike by surprise; he grinned, and shivered.

"Mike?"

"Mm?"

"I'll show you something, if you like."

"What?"

"Watch." In a second the flashlight was turned off and the cellar was deep in pitch darkness.

"Look up at the door," Liz was saying.

Mike stared blindly up. Veils of green and red drifted lazily across his vision, dragged into existence by even the slight change from flashlight to darkness. Gradually they cleared.

"Do you see it?"

"No. Where? What am I looking for?"

"Up where the door is. About halfway down."

Mike looked. "No. Not a thing."

There was an impatient shuffle of movement, and suddenly Liz was crouched next to him.

"Now. See?" Her small hands turned his face up towards the invisible wall opposite; higher than he had been looking.

"I think—yes, I can see it. What is it?"

There above them, faint but clearly recognizable now that he knew where to look, was a small gray light in the black firmament.

"It's the keyhole," Liz whispered, and her hands dropped from his face. Mike heard her slide back into her sleeping bag a moment later. "Don't you think it's rather nice to have a star in our sky?"

"A tarnished star," Mike replied.

"Yes," she agreed. "But it's better than nothing. And it looks as if it's so very far away."

Mike nodded. "I suppose it does."

The flashlight clicked on and the tiny speck of the early daylight outside winked out of existence.

"Don't tell anyone else," Liz said. "It's just for early morning people."

"OK." He thought for a while. "You know something?" he said, and at that moment Geoff's alarm clock clattered to life.

"Shut up, you little shit," Geoff moaned, and beat his arm against the clock. Frankie's hands appeared at the opening of her sleeping bag.

"Oh, God. What time is it?" she said.

There was the sound of children playing, down by the river; and the many different sounds of the woods itself, insects and birds and the humming of a thousand plants and trees warming in the sun. The path through the woods is wide and well-trodden, but there are ways that branch off it into the denser areas.

Sometimes, were it not for the regular passing of distant cars, the woods could almost become a forest, and the town outside it could vanish completely.

We were walking there because it was such a wonderful day to be outside, but also because there was a lot still to say; and this was a good way to go through it all.

"Go on," Mike said.

"It's not very easy.... The story goes back a long way, much further back than just at school or just down the Hole."

"Because of Martyn?"

"Yes. Simple, really. But again, very difficult. Because there's so much I can't find out, because there's no one to tell it. Lisa— well, that was something completely unexpected."

"Do I want to know what we got right?" he murmured, almost to himself.

"It won't be good news."

"I guessed it wouldn't be."

A scattering of blackbirds drew across the sky.

So in the end he told me, started to tell me—things.... I told you before, about where he grew up and all that. What he was like. He kept saying, I used to be so very different to what you see now; like it was something he had to explain. Like he was afraid I wouldn't understand. And I kept saying, OK, sure, go on ... you know ... because I didn't want him to stop—thinking about himself, not yet, in case he started talking about us, instead. So I kept saying, Go on, and saying, Yes, so that he would keep talking.

Sometimes he would stroke my hair and say how beautiful I was, and— all the time, he was—I don't know, getting more and more nervous, like he was afraid of something. It seemed ... I got the feeling that he was afraid of me, *which was so silly because all the time I was afraid of* him. *But it didn't happen all that often, just sometimes, and he never got beyond just touching my hair a little. But he used to talk, on and on, about—meaningless stuff, most of the time.*

He said his hobby was daydreaming, thinking of things, inventing things and so on. . . . I asked him what, but he laughed and said they were too grand for me—too grand for anyone, was what he said. As if they were things only he could understand. Maybe they were. His room was completely bare—nothing on the walls, no posters or anything, so maybe everything just went on in his head.

That woman—his aunt, you saw her, remember? She used to be around the house most of the time, and his uncle was there in the evenings. They treated him pretty much normally, I suppose . . . well, he did. She sometimes used to be—sort of hesitant. They were OK. I mean, they were nice enough people. They used to give me tea—like, Oh, are you Martyn's girlfriend? It was all nice and cozy, most of the time. I think they were pleased, really . . . you know, that he'd brought someone home to meet them, presentable middle-class girl from school. It was all really nice, for a while.

I didn't know anything about the Hole until it was actually happening. I promise that. I mean, if I'd known beforehand, I really would have told someone. It's not as though—I know that I saw a different side to Martyn than most people did, but I thought it was all pretty much under control . . . that he'd got himself under control. I didn't realize—what he might be capable of doing, until it was already happening.

He was always so popular, at school and so on. People were so keen to be with him, to be his friend. I felt almost—ungrateful, not being sure. Like the problem was me. Like I was imagining it, that what I thought was strange was really just normal. And everyone I knew—You're so lucky, *being his girl. He was never* mine, *you understand—it was never Martyn, Lisa's boyfriend. Always the other way . . . even when it was just girls talking about* us, I was always sort of tagged on to him. And everyone seemed to think I should be grateful to be tagged on. After a while it gets difficult to stop something like that, you know? There was nothing wrong with him at all, to begin with, I suppose. In all fairness . . . no, he was an all right guy. Really. It's just that, looking back to that beginning, I have to look past—what—

And I wasn't very strong, I suppose. I couldn't just turn around and walk off on a boy, not without a reason. And to begin with—shit, Liz—

To begin with, I think I thought . . . thought that I loved him. If you can believe that. I think I loved him, almost. Because it was so difficult not to be . . . swept along by him. . . . I really wanted to be that popular, that liked. And there he was, letting me. It was . . . wonderful, for a time . . . even with the times that he wasn't quite himself. Something showed through . . . something that was completely hidden, most of the time. But we were around each other so much. . . . He used to want to see me all the time, every day, every evening, looking at me, talking at me about things I didn't really understand—about life and what you make of it, about what he thought of so-and-so, who needed taking down a peg, who was—I don't know, who was next in line for one of his hellish jokes.

He never used to laugh at anything. . . . I remember thinking, He's too mature to laugh, he just makes the jokes and then sits back . . . but that wasn't it, I see now. I don't think he found any of it funny, do you understand? But if you call something a joke, then it's all right, isn't it? It was just a joke. Who gives a shit if that person has to leave because of it, it was funny at the time, right? And that scares me now. . . . Even if he had been caught, and everything had had to be found out, the Hole could just have been a joke that went wrong. Maybe . . . maybe that was a part of it. Test runs. Setting things up . . . he called it something, I don't remember what—a real joke, or something, the Hole. But none of it was really for fun.

And then suddenly it would slip a little . . . the image, the facade, would *get a bit thin one evening. . . . And then he would be stroking my hair, and talking, and looking at me, and all those things. Like he was waiting for something, or searching for something, who knows. Nothing more than that, but in his eyes—there, it was different—and I didn't understand any of it, not to begin with. I promise I would have told you, if I'd known. But he didn't tell me until—until that—*

I shut the tape recorder off. And found, despite the warmth and my own determination, that I was trembling.

"What would I be doing?" repeated Alex. "I don't know, really. The weather's OK. Maybe just lounging around."

"I'd be asleep," said Frankie. "It's still before noon. I can't believe how fanatic you guys are being about getting up."

"It's for your own good," Geoff said. "Otherwise you'd snore, and we'd pour water over you to shut you up, and then you'd be awake and wet, as well."

"Right."

"I think I'd quite like to be outside somewhere," Mike said. "In fact, after this is over, I'd feel good about climbing a mountain or two. Something nice and high up, anyway."

Alex nodded agreement. "It does make you feel that way," she said. "Like mild claustrophobia."

"This would be a nightmare if you were claustrophobic," Frankie said. "The walls! The walls are closing in on me!"

"Like in *Star Wars*," Geoff agreed.

"What?" Frankie said.

"This time last year I was in bed with the flu," Mike said. "Really bad flu. It was horrible."

"OK," said Alex. "This time last year I was in France."

"I thought you said you never went on holidays?" Geoff asked.

"Not with my family. Father's always zipping backwards and forwards between here and America, and Mum's got lots of stuff to do. Work and so on. France was with a friend of mine; we stayed at a crummy little auberge and bummed around for two weeks."

"Did you enjoy it?" Mike asked.

"Yeah. Very much. I like France—the way parts of it are ultramodern and parts are almost medieval."

"Sounds like my house," Mike muttered.

"Frankie?"

"Uh—this time last year I was—I can't remember. Hang on a bit." Frankie looked puzzled. "First week of the holidays . . . oh yeah, I know. It was party season, remember? All those parties we had to celebrate not being able to have sweet sixteen parties any more."

"So what parties *did* you have?" Geoff asked. He was pulling a thread from the knee of his jeans with careful deliberation.

"I don't know . . . yes I do. We had a late New Year party." Frankie giggled. "We all went up to London and danced about in Trafalgar Square and all that crap."

"Who is this?" asked Mike.

"Oh, me and Kate and Jim Stevens and Alice and Dobbs and all that lot."

"Oh, *that* lot," Mike said.

"What's that supposed to mean?" Frankie demanded.

"A group of people with but one thing in common," Geoff said. "Their desire to achieve status as human beings."

"Fuck off, Geoff," Frankie said. "I ought to get that printed on little cards so I could just give you one instead of saying it. Save time."

"The amount of times you tell Geoff to fuck off, it would cost a fortune," Mike said.

"What about Geoff?" Alex asked, tactfully. "What were you up to?"

"Me? What?"

"Where were you this time last year?"

Geoff shrugged. "You know. Around."

"Spill it, Geoff," Mike said.

"Well, I think it was about this time that terrorists stole our house and we had to call in Uncle George to sort them out. Uncle George used to be in the SAS, but they threw him out because he was too rough."

Mike smiled. "Seriously, though." Geoff shrugged again.

"I don't know. Doing sweet nothing, probably. I don't seem to have as crammed a social calendar as you guys."

"I was in bed with flu," Mike reminded him.

"At least you had your microbes for company."

"I bet you did something more exciting than that, in any case," Alex said.

"I don't know. Maybe I did. Must have been bloody memorable."

"Liz?" Alex asked.

"I was on top of my shed," Liz said.

"What, all Easter?"

"No. Right now. I built a shed in the garden. I was putting roofing felt on it."

"On your own?" Mike asked.

"Nobody else but li'l ol' me," Liz affirmed.

"You built a *shed*?" Alex said. "That's pretty impressive."

"Sounds like you had nearly as good a time as I had," Geoff said.

"It was nice," Liz said. "It's still there. Something I built."

"You do a lot of stuff, don't you?" Frankie remarked. "All that cooking, and now building things. I didn't realize you got up to so much."

"You get used to it," Liz said shortly.

"What are we doing for lunch?" Mike asked. For some indefinable reason, he felt as though the conversation had moved towards something which Liz found uncomfortable.

"Aha! The Appetite rears its ugly head once more," Geoff said.

"Just as long as it's not bits of ham again," Alex said.

That evening was good; a bright time in the long span of the Hole. We found ourselves talking about what we hoped to do with our lives, which is a happy subject; unhindered by foresight or prescience, we were able to view the future as an open, welcoming world into which we would stroll with complete awareness. If life was like this, in reality, it would be easy; and, I suspect, dull.

The illusion of free will is in fact only the shadow of our own ignorance about the future. It seems ridiculous to assume that the future is in our hands, and subject to our whims, simply because we are not yet privy to its shape and nature. Nothing has changed from one day to the next except our viewpoint. Along the single line we experience as time, it is only our perspective that moves; and why should a perspective change anything?

I do not think we will ever see the future.

I never thought about the way we look at things until Martyn forced me to; Martyn, and the others in the Hole. And, of course, when you start examining things like that, the method sticks in your brain and is there forever—so that every comment or assumption, every prejudice and bias is registered and subject to questioning. Very healthy, sure. But also very hard to live with. It's a painful kind of ability to force on yourself.

Something about here and now. When I set the notebook down, rest my arm or go downstairs to eat or drink, the Hole recedes just a little—like a TV cross-fade—and normal life reasserts itself, sharp and clean. But here, when I sit down in this old attic, it's all very close to me again. I feel it growing, up here; swelling to fill this room as I write it out again.

And while these words dry into immutability on the page, I hear the slam of a garage door somewhere and the radio in the kitchen where my mother is; and night air begins to draw past the half-open attic window, as the trees light up in the falling sun. It is a cool, long, wide summer evening, and the grass has turned blue-gray in the dusk. Sitting here I can see a tracery of clouds, high up in the sky. And at this time, the Hole is centuries away, and might even belong to someone else.

FIVE

Day three: the last day of the Hole.

"Good old English block," Mike said at lunchtime, patting the wall behind his shoulder. "I sure will miss it."

"I've been sitting here so long I'm practically a fixture," Alex said.

Frankie, lying on her front and kicking her legs in the air, fumbled around in a pocket of a discarded top and triumphantly brandished a small lump of something.

"Aha! Last bit of Turkish delight," she crowed happily. "I knew it was here somewhere."

"Christ, Frankie," said Geoff in amazement. "It's gone gray."

Frankie peered at it. "That's OK. This bit was lemon-flavored to begin with."

"Yuck," Mike said. "I can't say it looks too appetizing, Frankie."

"Well, did you hear that?" Geoff asked. "Mike doesn't like the look of it. Must be pretty putrid."

"Mike the Molars," Alex said, with a smile.

Mike opened his mouth.

"No fillings," he said indistinctly.

"But not through lack of trying," Geoff added.

Lunch, which they cooked late on the last cylinder of camping gas, was canned meatballs and a variety of odds and ends from everybody's knapsacks. They ate it while talking; they seemed to have much to talk about.

At three o'clock, Geoff raised an arm.

"Does anyone have anything to drink?" he asked.

"Mm—I have some lemonade, I think," Liz said. Geoff looked sideways at her.

"I meant alcoholic," he said.

"Oh," said Liz. Nobody had. Geoff reached behind his knapsack where it was leaned against the wall and drew out a bottle of vodka and a lemon.

"I've been saving this for when we ran out," he said. "It's for a kiss-the-booze-goodbye party."

Mike looked heavenward. "This twat's even brought a lemon," he complained. "Drinking's a vocation with you, isn't it?"

"It's an art form," Geoff said sagely.

"And a vocation's a holiday," Alex said.

"Ha," Mike said dismally. "The woman is a wit."

They mixed the vodka with Liz's lemonade and passed cups round.

"Well, hello," he had said.

I had been sitting behind second arch, on the old bench there. The field trip minibus, with its complement of ardent field trippers, had set off a little under an hour ago; I had watched it draw away from the tarmac square in front of the cricket pavilion.

Martyn was pink and looked rather surprised to see me. He dropped a big carrier bag by the arch and came over to where I was sitting. "You're early. We don't start until five."

"Is the stopwatch running?" I asked.

"I'm not *that* fanatic," he said. "What have you been doing?"

"I just saw off the field trip," I explained.

The reaction was alarming. He stopped dead, and a look of confusion and anger swept across his face in the instant before he asked, quickly. "Did they *see* you?"

"Of course not."

"You're sure?"

"Yes. I was over here all the time."

He seemed to relax a little. "Good. Only, it would be . . . very bad, if anyone had seen you. Screw things up no end."

"I know," I said. "Which is why I stayed out of sight."

A slow smile spread over his features.

"Fine. Yes—we want to keep this quiet, this little project. It would *not* do for Carter or Arkwright to twig as to the goings-on I'm planning."

"Which are?"

He laughed. "Wait and see, as almost everybody's grand-mother used to say." He sat down on the bench and stuck his legs out. Fair hair spilled over one eye and he blew upwards, making it fan out.

"Not that Carter ever notices anything I do," said Mar-tyn. "In a way, it's even a little annoying that he never suspects me. He always thinks it's the louts from the other side of the quad. Too set in his ways by miles."

"In what way?"

"He still thinks that the problem kids are the ones in tatty leather jackets who get caught smoking and talk at the back of class. The sort who used to make spitballs at prep school and chuck them at the ceiling. Thirty years ago he might have been right, I suppose."

"So you class yourself as one of the new breed of school rebel?"

He laughed and shrugged. "The perfect rebel is like the perfect criminal. He's not the guy everyone knows about. He's the kid who does his work, hands in his essays on time, is polite and never gets caught. As with reference to myself and our friend Carter, who thinks that the sun shines out of the seat of my trousers. Clean trousers, note, with creases."

I nodded, understanding. "But the whole school knows about you," I said.

"Oh, I'm not the perfect rebel by a long way," he said casually. "Just a hobby, right?"

"Right," I said, confused; it was a joke, but he hadn't said it as a joke. "So what's the perfect crime, then?"

Martyn frowned, as if he'd never thought about it.

"The crime no one even knows about," he said at last.

"That's how I had it, too," I agreed.

And looking back, I see a mistake here—a minor slip that slid past me at the time. He thought a moment too long before answering. The answer was correct; it was the right thing to say; but Martyn was far too bright to need even three seconds or so to work out what to say. The careful thought had been a sham, for he had known the answer long before I asked the question.

"I get the feeling," he went on, "that people like Carter can't even acknowledge the possibility of something happening if they haven't heard about it. Mr. Carter has his finger on the pulse of this school, as he is so fond of telling us. He's been here thirty years; he knows. But then things happen, and there's no one to blame. What does poor Mr. Carter do? The same as our estimable Mr. Arkwright, or even old Gibbon, rest his bones. He does nothing, because he cannot recognize any other options. Sad, really."

"So," I said. "What advice would you give to the would-be rebel?"

"Think big," he said at once. "Half-hearted stuff gets you expelled."

"Big, like the End of Term Address?"

"Exactly. And it's a matter of personality, as well. I knew that Arkwright wouldn't even look for a culprit, because to start some sort of investigation would be a clear admission to the truth of the veiled accusation that the sheep represented."

"Own up whoever is attempting to slander Mr. Law," I said.

"Yes. So he treated it as a joke, and laughed it off. Who knows? Maybe he didn't even realize it was directed at Law. Perhaps the old bat was truly bemused by the whole incident. It wouldn't be the first time that things have happened at Our Glorious School which he hasn't been able to figure out." He spoke with a hard and happy dismissiveness.

"I pity whichever university gets you," I said lightly.

"Ah," he said. His voice was well-modulated and easy. "I don't think so. I think practical jokes are on the way out."

"Moving on?"

"Indeed."

I thought about that. "So what is the Hole?"

"Oh, it's not a joke. Far from that. Didn't I say? It's an experiment—"

"—with real life," I finished. "You did say."

"Something a bit different. Yes."

We looked up at the sound of footsteps. Geoff turned the corner and saw us. "Hi, guys. I hear it's party time."

"I hope you're suitably equipped?" Martyn enquired.

"You obviously haven't heard the rumors," Geoff said. "What have you got in there?"

"That," said Martyn, "is a rope ladder. An integral part of our little adventure."

"Sounds kinky," Geoff said.

At four o'clock, with only an hour of the Hole remaining, the atmosphere became increasingly relaxed. Mike, having drunk more of Geoff's surprise vodka than he had initially intended, sat encased in a warm glow of goodwill that embraced everything. The vodka, when mixed with lemonade, tasted like lemonade. He'd had four mugs of the mixture, and was halfway down his fifth, matching Geoff and Frankie. After all, he told himself, in an hour it would all be over. He frowned: climbing the rope ladder might be a bit tricky.

Alex was smiling at him, he realized.

"Mikey, you look awfully drunk," she said.

"I do?"

"Yes."

"I do. How's that?"

"You have a sort of—well, you have a certain slipped-sideways look to you."

Mike assumed an expression of contempt. "That," he said, "is probably your vision becoming blurred."

Alex laughed. "Could be," she admitted.

"Who's the best egg?" Frankie said, loudly.

"What the fuck are you talking about?" Geoff said.

"Good eggs," Frankie said. "Mike's a good egg. Alex is a good egg. Frankie is an *awfully* good egg. But who is the *best* egg?"

"Who rattled your cage?" Alex said.

"Don't ask," Mike said.

"I object to the expression 'good egg' on the grounds that it's bloody annoying," Geoff said.

"I think Liz is a good egg," decided Mike.

"Thanks," said Liz. "What qualities do you look for in a good egg?"

Mike pondered this.

Geoff said, "Good legs and a sense of adventure."

"That's not a good egg," Mike said. "That's a good lay. Ha! Joke!"

"Our dog's got nice legs and a sense of adventure," Alex said. "Says a lot for your taste in women, Geoff."

"She's maligning me again," he complained.

"Did my joke come out all right?" Mike asked.

"Probably as well as could be expected, given the circumstances," Liz told him.

There are pencils and pens in the jar in front of me. I often wonder why we still live in this huge old house, stuck back in the trees away from the village. The river cuts through the woods about a quarter of a mile out. The river is something I like very much; I was there again yesterday, walking around to the stand of chestnuts. But the house puzzles me, I suppose. The first floor and the attic are places that only I see, of course; and they have become like I am, in the fashion that places take after their occupants. So my mother's room, past the kitchen, is blue and neat and fresh, with watercolors on the walls and a single slender vase on the windowsill, while my room is a tumble of browns and ochres, autumn colors that light up fiercely in the sun. Stacked around the skirting are the various portions of my past, hidden away in shoe boxes and tied-up plastic bags. My window faces the opposite way to the attic; I can sit on my bed and see the river trees, with no buildings in sight at all.

Anyway, while I was walking, I met someone that it seemed I hadn't seen in a very long time.

"Oh," she said. "Hi." Strange to see how we become strangers to each other so easily.

"Hi, Alex," I said.

"You just out walking?"

I smiled at that. "It would seem so," I admitted. And all of a sudden I felt very sorry for her, standing there unsure of what to say, uncomfortable, facing a person that she was both grateful to and afraid of. "Come on," I said. "Let's go and get a Coke or something. We could talk about things."

Too quickly, she replied, "Like what?"

"What you're doing with yourself, for example. I haven't seen much of you for a while."

She smiled gratefully. "I'd like that. Uh—isn't there an ice-cream truck at the parking lot?"

"Jim. Yeah, he's always there about this time of day."

I went and bought the Cokes and we sat down under a big old beech tree, in the shade.

"And?" I asked.

"I don't know." She was much more comfortable now. "I think we're moving to a new house pretty soon."

"That's sad," I said. "We'd all miss you, you know."

She laughed, but without much humor. "Sure, likewise. But I won't mind all that much. There's not a lot around here for me now. When you see this place from the outside, you realize just how ... cramped, and small, it really is. I won't be sorry."

The shared experience of the Hole stood in the background of our conversation like a ghost, and every word we said was tainted by its presence. There is never any going back, not when something's done. It wasn't too long before we made our excuses and moved apart again, ensuring that the necessary words were exchanged.

And, just for a moment, I felt like shouting out across the parking lot in front of the hot women with baby carriage-bound children, and the fat bald men, "I saved your life! Haven't you got more to say to me than that?"

And then I felt very ashamed.

• • •

"What time is it?" asked Alex.

"Time for a refill," said Geoff. "This is the last, folks, so make the most of it."

"Sure," Mike said happily. He felt very relaxed, indeed. In fact, he thought idly, he might even be getting close to being silly. Silly was what Geoff said: "Got a bit silly and fell over a bicycle," or "Got silly last night and fell asleep on the floor in Vernon's room." Silly might well, he decided, be a good place to be.

"I'm not sure that's wise, Mikey," Alex said. "You've had a lot of that stuff."

"Whoa, my conscience speaks," Mike said. "Amazing. An—a separate entity, my conscience. Exo-conscience."

"He's talking in tongues," Frankie said.

"Mike's a big boy, he can look after himself," Geoff said.

"What time is it?" Alex asked again.

"It's a quarter to six," Geoff said. "Or, if you look at it like *this*, it's about nine o'clock. And if you turn it this way, it's— well, you can't see too easily, because it's facing down."

"Martyn's late," Liz said.

"Who said he'd come at five o'clock?" Mike said. The idea of Martyn being late did not seem a particularly important one. "It doesn't have to be exactly three days, does it? He'll turn up in a bit. Something always turns up," he added.

"It should have been five o'clock," Alex said. "We went down at five."

"He's having his—tea," said Frankie.

"That's a point," Mike said. "I'm all for a curry. Let's have a curry or something."

"It'll have to be something, I'm afraid," Geoff said.

"I've got some candy bars and a pack of spaghetti that you add boiling water to," Alex said.

"Never mind," Mike said. "Never mind."

And time continued to pass them by.

I forget who actually said it first. But someone must have, because we all knew it before long. So maybe it was Alex; let us put the words into her mouth.

"He's not going to come, is he," Alex said. It was not even a question.

It could have been Alex. The certainty was abruptly there with us, and there was little we could do to shift it. But it was not until later that the full realization began to sink in; at first, we only knew that Martyn was not coming. Beyond that we did not look. I think we expected him sometime early the next day, perhaps, when he had sorted out whatever had waylaid him. That's what we thought, at first.

And then it occurred to one or two of us that this was the theatrical element in Martyn's plan, that this was the joke behind the Hole. And these people found themselves rather pleased that they had so easily seen through what appeared to be a simplistic and really quite obvious twist to the end of the Hole.

And when it was time to sleep, we slept. And sleep is a curious time for us, because whatever barriers we have drop away; and we are left free to walk our fears and fantasies, even those from which we are protected during our waking lives. We slept that night, and in that sleep came crawling up the—other certainties. And with them came that primordial fear of the dark.

I don't remember my dreams. Not many people do. So maybe I was happy and carefree in my sleep; I don't know. But I do know that I lay awake for a long time, and in that time the darkness of the Hole was split occasionally by the sounds of the nightmares of those who slept about me.

Six

I finished writing for that afternoon, stacked the notebooks and closed the window. It was the hot, lazy kind of day when people sunbathe or sit in the shade sipping cool drinks from long glasses, or walk beneath trees. Summer is an unreal time of year, linked to our book-born images of England and fair weather. And when it comes—if it comes—it can make the trivialities of everyday life swim away into its shallow heat haze.

I shut the door on the flat reincarnation of the Hole and stepped into the bright driveway. The air was thick as I went out, away from the village, on the wide road that curls up to the chestnut and beech woods that fronts Our Glorious School. Deserted, of course; the empty classrooms settling in their chalk dust, smelling of burlap and stone.

It was five o'clock already. Mike was waiting when I reached fifth arch, looking the wrong way; dark hair and a crappy old jacket which didn't suit him at all. I smiled as I walked up behind him.

"Hi," he said, and turned round.

"I didn't think you'd heard me," I said. "Hi, yourself."

"You look good. And it's good to see you, too. I'm not see-ing enough of you."

"You mean you could cope with more?"

"Surely. How's the—writing going?"

"Slowly. But it'll be over before the summer is, I hope."

"Good." He said it firmly. "I don't know what to call it. A story? Sounds too innocent. A study of the mind of Martyn? Could you live with a title like that?"

"No," I said. "It's not all about Martyn, either. That's just part of it."

"The most important part of it."

I smiled. "Perhaps. Other things happened as well, you know."

"So they did."

We walked down past the groundsman's shed, past the cricket pavilion towards the woods. As we did, I tried to imagine that I was walking alone away from the Hole, having just shut the door on five people. I knew what I was doing; I knew what was going to happen to them all. What did that make me? A psychopath, perhaps. But that word is far too blunt a term to come close to describing Martyn. He was like a brilliant scien-tist for whom the troubles of the world are of little concern, bending over a petri dish of tiny creatures which cannot escape from their curved prison. He knows they will die, but it does not matter to him; he will learn something from the pattern of their struggles and death throes, and, after all, they are only tiny creatures. The loss of tiny creatures cannot be a great one; it is not comparable to the loss of a person. And Martyn only recognized the existence of one person. He was completely alone in his universe.

"I want to go to America," Mike was saying. "I've always wanted to."

"Can I come?" I said.

"I was hoping you would."

"Really? You're really going to America?"

"Yeah. Soon. Before university. We could earn ourselves some money, bum around."

"Doing what?"

"Who cares?" He sighed. "You could write it all down, if you want to. There's not always a need for a reason."

I said, "I really do love you, don't I?"

"Getting rhetorical on me? Of course, I'm not sure that being loved by you is safe. You being so like Martyn, and so on."

It was my turn to sigh. "Yes. That was it, wasn't it? The twist. Quite a twist, too—to write my own way out of the Hole, I mean. . . ."

"Quite a twist," he agreed. "And Martyn never saw it coming until it hit him."

"He would have done, if he hadn't been so sure of himself," I said.

"Sorry?"

"If he'd thought, even for a moment, that his plan was less than perfect, then he might have started looking for ways to see through the bluff. But because he was utterly confident in it—in himself, I suppose—then he couldn't imagine that I had found a gap. And so he fell for it."

Mike laughed uneasily. "That sounds convincing. I think."

"He never thought we could be a threat. No more than God would be afraid of men hunting him down and killing him. Excuse the simile."

"I've seen too much to make any claims about God," Mike said. "Maybe that's wisdom."

"Knowing so much that you can't decide on anything?"

"No. Not really."

"I know."

"And where is our . . . demi-god, now?"

"Gone away."

"Forever, I hope."

"I'm not so sure," I said. Martyn wouldn't just vanish; not that easily.

"What do you mean? You don't think he'd come back—for revenge, or something?"

"No. I think he's finished with us. But that doesn't mean he's just going to lie down and fade away. I think one day, Martyn will have something to say to the world. Maybe forty years from now."

"At least he's a safe distance away," Mike said.

"Safe? I doubt that. Gods of any sort aren't safe." I stepped carefully over an exposed root. "I'll be watching for him, believe me. That's something we should all do."

We had entered the flecked shade at the outskirts of the woods, where insects bobbed and whirled in hazy clouds in the heat. Mike pushed up his sleeves.

"What worries me is that he'll have learned from us," he said. "He'll do it better next time, whatever it turns out to be."

"Yes," I agreed. "That scares me, too. But what else could we do?"

"We could have turned him in to the police," Mike said. "He's a murderer, isn't he?"

"Not quite," I said, and the irony made me smile. "He's just a schoolboy who got mixed up in a silly prank. And nobody got hurt, did they? Nobody died. You can't have a murder without bodies. And all the corpses are walking around looking suspiciously alive."

Mike started to say something, and then checked himself. "Yeah. That's what they'd say. I know that." Then he seemed to change his mind. "But he's mad, Liz. Couldn't they see that?"

I turned to face him, the warmth of the woods humming around us. "We didn't," I reminded him. "No, they'd never see what we saw. You had to be there. . . . Martyn's a perfectly normal guy. A bright, articulate, charismatic guy who just happens to think he's God and that other people are playthings."

"It's a nightmare," he said hollowly.

"He could have been great," I said. "He could yet. Do you know what Carter wrote on his report at the end of his last term? I have the greatest confidence that Martyn will make the most of his many skills. He will without a doubt go far." I giggled. "Do you think Hitler got school reports like that?"

"Not funny," Mike said.

"I know. Which is why I'm laughing. Hey, murder—let's not take it too seriously, OK?"

He stared at me in silence for a moment, and then a wide grin broke across his face.

"You're crazy," he said, and turned, and kissed me slowly. I gripped the back of his jacket in my hands, hands turned to fists, and held him hard against me for a long time.

And then we went on in silence, crossed the stream where it ambled through the trees. Soon we were on the footpath that cuts down to the main road. Behind us, one or two towers of Our Glorious School could be seen jutting, gray and small, above the summer-green leaves of the woods. We made leisurely progress down to the village heading for the Horseman where the beer-garden tables would already be seating the evening's first customers.

"What will you have?" Mike asked, when we'd arrived.

"Anything. Doesn't matter."

He ordered a pint and a glass of orange juice, and the guy behind the bar gave them to us the wrong way round. We swapped and went outside.

"Here's to murderers," Mike said. We sat in the gently mellowing sunlight and drank quietly.

Mike awoke strangling, stifled by some great weight that only lifted when he sat up gasping. The nightmare drifted away and he was alone in the silence of the Hole. Vague tendrils of the dream still lingered at the back corners of his mind, but he could not catch hold of them. Gradually the sensation ebbed.

It must be the fourth day. The day that no one had expected. Mike smiled wryly into the darkness; trust Martyn to pull something like this. Then the smile faded as he became more awake, more aware of the fact that he felt sick. For one wild moment he imagined himself badly ill in the Hole, unable to get help, trapped by Martyn's stupid prank which had suddenly turned serious. And then he remembered the party the day before, and how drunk he had got. The sickness was a hangover; nothing more. He was mildly reassured.

Wondering whether it was daytime yet, or still the middle of the night, he searched the empty sky of the Hole for the small gray star Liz had discovered. It was there where he had seen it last, a single point of dull light. He wished that it were brighter; but of course the doorway to the Hole was towards the end of a short passage, and sunlight would never strike the keyhole directly.

"Mike?" It was Geoff's voice.

"Yeah?"

"What time is it? Should we get up yet?"

"I don't know. It's daytime outside."

"Shit." There was a pause, and he heard Geoff turning around inside his sleeping bag. "I think we'd better turn the light on."

"OK."

The bulb snapped on, and the crack of the intense light made Mike start with surprise. The repetitive pulse of a headache began to pull together at the base of his skull.

"You look fucking awful," Geoff said.

"I don't feel too good, either."

"Drink some water."

Alex struggled upright. "What's going on?"

"It's time to get up," Geoff said. "Well, nearly. Half-past seven."

"Still here," Frankie said indistinctly. "I thought maybe it was just a bad dream and I'd wake up at home."

"Fat chance," Geoff said. "Seriously, Mike. Get some water inside you. You'll feel a lot better."

"Maybe you're right," Mike said. He got unsteadily to his feet and went round the corner to the lavatory. Cupping his hands under the twisting stream of water from the tap, he washed his neck and face briefly and then gulped down seven or eight mouthfuls. The water was cold and tasted metallic. Below his feet, the distant thrumming of the drain echoed faintly up through the grating in the floor. He straightened, shook his head. When he got back to the other room everyone was awake and sitting up. The conversation quickly centered on Martyn.

"This is bloody ridiculous," Frankie said. "I've got better things to do than hang around down here. And my parents will be furious if I don't show up."

"They're not going to know until next week, though," Geoff reminded her. Frankie stopped, taken aback.

"I'd forgotten that," she said. She sounded puzzled.

"Where is he?" Alex said. "It is a bit much. I thought this was going to be quite good up till now. It's just childish."

"He's probably just wanting to see how we react," Geoff said casually. "It's bound to be part of the experiment. We'll go over it all at great length in the—what was it?"

"Debriefing," Alex supplied, "At least, that's what he called it."

"Mike looks pretty this morning," Frankie added. "Hadn't noticed until now. What a sight!"

"Thank you," Mike said. "That makes me feel really good."

"Are you OK?" Liz asked. Mike was pleased to hear that she sounded genuinely concerned.

"Too much of Geoff's vodka stuff," he said quickly. "I'll live."

"I have some—here. Have an aspirin."

Mike raised one eyebrow, but took the proffered bottle of tablets. "Where did these come from?"

"Oh," Liz said. "I just thought we'd probably need them."

"You haven't by any chance got a twelve-foot ladder and a crowbar in that knapsack?" Geoff asked. "Only if you have, please don't wait to be asked. We could get out right now." Nobody laughed.

Then Alex said, "I've got it!" The others stared at her. "Why he isn't here," she explained. "It's obvious. I mean, everyone agrees that it's not like Martyn to do something as silly as not letting us out on time. It's not his style. That's the sort of thing kids do when they're six; shut someone in a cupboard and won't open the door. Right?"

"Yeah," Geoff agreed cautiously. "So?"

"So what was the original idea?" Alex said. "We were to come down here for three days, and then get together at Martyn's house for the rest of the week to talk about it. How we really got to know each other and all that. He'd keep us all out of sight at his place until the legitimate Peak District expedition gets back. But what happens if, for some reason, he can't take us back to his house? Something simple, like a friend comes round that evening unexpectedly. That's all it is, betcha. He's just waiting until it's absolutely safe to let us out."

Geoff thought about it. "Makes sense," he admitted. "Yeah, there's probably a good enough reason. I couldn't believe Martyn would stick us down here for no reason except as a corny joke."

"His jokes have never been corny before," Frankie said.

"Well, that's all right then," Mike said. "We'll just hang around a bit."

"Not much else we can do," Alex said. "I'm hungry. What's left to eat?"

They gathered together the packs of food that hadn't yet been used up.

"Thank goodness Mike eats so much," Frankie said cheerfully. "I brought all this extra crap to compensate."

"Backhanded compliment if ever I heard one," Mike told her. He didn't know if he was imagining the effects of the aspirin, but the headache had receded and he felt a lot better.

"There's nothing really breakfasty here," Alex said. "Sorry. There's a sort of boil-in-the-bag lasagna, if anyone wants that. Mike?"

"I don't think I'm quite up to eating yet," Mike said.

"All the more for the rest of us."

"Hey," said Liz. "Actually, mightn't it be better to keep some stuff back? Just in case—in case he doesn't get here before lunch?"

"Nah. What's one meal?" Geoff said. "You can always have an extra large supper."

"Well, yes. But he might not be here by supper, either," Liz said uncomfortably.

"What are you trying to say?"

"Only that we don't know when he might be able to make it. So don't rush things; the food may have to stretch a little further than we imagine."

Geoff shrugged. "He won't be long. Come on. There are two sausages left."

• • •

It was a Saturday evening; about seven o'clock, just after people started arriving. Everyone was there . . . you know the crowd, Jill and Alex and the guys from second arch. We stood around—there weren't all that many people dancing yet. We stood by the bar and sipped drinks and laughed a lot. I'd gone there with Natasha and some friends of hers. She was really big on London, always going on about the parties and clubs and so on. I was pleased . . . because I was new, and it was good to be with everyone else. I was pleased Natasha liked me, as well.

"Flying Angels for Lisa and me," she told the man behind the bar. "You've got to meet some people," she said to me. "They'll all be here, of course; everyone worth knowing, anyway."

"Who's worth knowing?" I asked. She listed a whole lot of people, I don't remember them all.

"Martyn might be here," she said. I'd heard all about Martyn, of course, but I hadn't actually seen him then. He sometimes turns up, when the mood takes him. I had an idea of what he'd be like, though . . . a tall boy, elegant, with dark eyes and a sort of arrogant sneer.

We went and joined a group near where the band had started playing. Vernon was there. "Hey! Who's this?" he said.

Natasha said, "This is Lisa. She's my latest discovery. Quite wonderful."

"Hello, Lisa," Vernon said, kidding around like mad, and kissed my hand. "Congratulations on being discovered. . . ."

I said thanks, or something. This was all outside what I was used to. I tried to join in all the jokes . . . but when you don't know what they're all aimed at, it's not so easy. People know when you're trying to fit in. Anyway. Then this . . . this new guy came up, looking just about as lost as I felt. He hung around on the edge of the group for a while, and then eased his way through and sat down next to where I was standing. Then he looked up at me—I don't know, he sort of froze there . . . didn't move, didn't say anything. As if I was really strange or he knew me from somewhere else. And then Vernon said, "Hi, Martyn."

Natasha said, "This is Lisa. Lisa, meet Martyn, our resident wacky dude."

Vernon said, "Martyn is one crazy shit-head," which everyone found pretty funny.

I must have looked really surprised, because he suddenly smiled— Martyn, that is—Martyn suddenly smiled at me and said, "I take the black mask off on weekends, you know." But his eyes were still thoughtful, and he was still looking at me. I guessed what he'd said was a joke, so I laughed. So this was him, I was thinking. He doesn't look anything like I thought he would.

Then one of the other boys said, "Let us retire to the bar once again," and some of them made off across the dance floor.

"Well," Martyn said. "A new face among the London crowd. Always a welcome sight."

"Are these things good?" I asked.

He said, "That depends what you get your kicks from," or something like that.

I thought he meant that he wasn't keen on it all, so I said, "I don't like big parties all that much, actually."

"So why are you here?" he asked immediately.

I said, "Natasha said I should come," which sounded really silly, and I giggled, and he smiled, too.

"You should never do what people expect you to," he said, mock-serious. "Living up to expectations and stereotypes cramps a person's style."

I could see that Natasha was waving to me across the hall. I said, "I'll see you around, I expect."

"Yes," he said. "Enjoy your evening." Then, as I was about to go away, he added, "I'd like to talk to you . . . when we've both got more time. You—you remind me of someone I knew once."

I nodded quickly and went away. It felt good; that I'd just met the most envied boy in the school, and he'd said he wanted to talk to me some time. I had a really good evening, because I didn't feel like I was just one of Natasha's hangers-on any more . . . it was like I'd suddenly become a proper person.

I stopped the machine and sat back. The question is, would anyone else have reacted differently? I shouldn't think so. Martyn was—is—an incredibly charismatic person.

But the thing that stays with me most, that scares me most, is what I did. Listening to Lisa's voice, recorded onto thin magnetic tape a long time ago, it is starkly apparent that I can never say sorry, never take it back or make it right. And that is what hurts. That is what still hurts.

SEVEN

It became lunchtime. Mike, having missed even the meager breakfast shared by the others, found himself painfully hungry.

"I'm not sure—" Alex began.

"What?"

"Well. Is it wise to finish this stuff off? Maybe we should—save some of it. For this afternoon."

"What's left?" Mike asked. "Shit, I'm hungry."

"You're just going to have to learn to live on the same amounts as the rest of us get," Frankie said. "I'm not having anyone eat half my share, as well."

"There's no need to worry," Alex said quickly. "Everything will be fair." She sorted her way through the small pile of packets by her side. "Here. This is all I've got."

"Of course there's need to worry," Geoff said. "Pretty soon this is going to stop being even faintly amusing. I don't know about the rest of you, but I'm bored shitless."

"We know," said Frankie. "We've heard it before. Doesn't make any difference, though, does it? So just sit there and be bored."

Mike found all the food he had left in his knapsack and placed it in a row on the floor in front of him. The others had all done something similar.

"There's not very much, is there?" Alex said in a small voice.

"We'll have to eat it a little at a time," Frankie said.

They sorted out a portion of the food for each of them and ate, thoughtfully.

"It would be interesting, if this was real," Geoff said. "If you were in a desert or on an island, with not much to eat. What would you do?"

"Thankfully, we're not on an island," Alex said.

"You could catch fish and stuff on an island," Mike said brightly. "And boil them gently in freshwater pools in the sun at midday, or bake them on hot rocks from a camp fire."

"Shut up," Frankie said. "Stop talking about food."

"Yeah, Mikey," Alex said.

"I'm sorry."

"It's just not very tactful right now."

"OK, OK."

The afternoon began, and the group was quiet for a while. Mike, lying on his back with his arms crossed, stared at the door at the top of the opposite wall and thought about what might be happening outside it. The big holly bush at the top of the stairway would perhaps be moving a little in the wind, and the sun would maybe be shining brightly on the empty cricket pitches and worn-down flagstones of the quad. The shadows of the arches would have begun their stately procession across the paths and lawns of the walk to the English block, where they would stretch and elongate as the afternoon grew old.

He wondered what the Peak District expedition was doing. Three more days and they would be back. He looked around the Hole at the others. Liz was holding the empty lemonade bottle and fiddling idly with the cap. An expression of mild concern passed briefly across her face. The cap came off, and she carefully replaced it and set the bottle down. She glanced up and caught Mike's gaze, and smiled at him, before picking up the notebook she always had nearby, and leafing through it. Mike wondered what she wrote down in there.

Martyn didn't make mistakes. The thought appeared in his head without volition, as if neatly placed there. He examined it. In all the previous exploits that Martyn had been involved with, there had never been any screw-ups like this. That was the whole point of Martyn's plans: they worked like the precision mechanism of a bomb—accurately, and unnoticeably until the exact moment of detonation. Martyn had never made mistakes before.

It wasn't a good thought, and Mike had almost turned it aside and forgotten it when something else came into his mind. If this wasn't a mistake, then it was either deliberate or something had happened to Martyn. The weight of that bore down on him, and it was about that moment that he first began to see how near to God Martyn had become.

The river, near to the bend that takes it past the edge of the common, turns fat and full for a while. The water there is deep, and the banks are thick with sedge and the long ears of wild grass. At dusk, as the air had just begun to be mild after the strong heat of the day, I went down to the river and swam.

Diving down it becomes dark and heavy. There are long arms of waterweed which lap at your legs and arms, twisting slowly in the current. I held my breath and swam far out under the water, into the middle of the flow. Our river is too old to be dangerous; it doesn't sweep people up and carry them off to the sea. Just a little way further down, by the ford, the young moms gather in the afternoon with toddlers who splash about on the clean gravel that lines the riverbed. But where I was, the bottom of the river is still mud, and the weeds still grow, and I like to imagine that the current could be deadly.

I surfaced, and made languidly for the far bank. Looking up, the edges of the sky had turned almost transparent; a thin haze of the palest green-white circled everything I could see. Looking straight up from the middle of the river you can see nothing at all but sky; and with your ears under water and no birds in sight, there might be nothing else at all. I turned, and swam steadily across at an angle, making up the ground that I had lost to the gentle movement of the river. It was summer, and I knew that in summer the teeth of any river are drawn for a while. But the first storm after the drought—well, you would never go swimming then. Or perhaps you might—but only if you were crazy or desperate.

I pulled myself out at the sharp rise of the bank, feeling the water draw down my body. The bite of the air was there instantly, and I shivered, waiting a time before reaching for the towel so that I could taste it and enjoy it. At home, only ten minutes away at a brisk walk, there would be hot tea. I smiled, toweled myself to a quick warmth and dragged on jeans and a sweatshirt. I was damp all over, of course, an uncomfortable way to walk home. It didn't really matter.

"He simply doesn't make mistakes," Mike said again. "So this is either deliberate or something's happened to him."

"Such as what?"

"I don't know. Suppose he broke a leg or something, and had to go to hospital. He could be gone for weeks."

"But that—" Alex said, and stopped.

"That wouldn't happen to Martyn?" Geoff finished for her. His voice was harsh. "Of course it might. What did you think? That Martyn won't let nasty things happen to him?" He slammed his palm down on the floor. "Shit. Nobody even knows we're here."

"What are we going to do?" Frankie said.

"It might not be that at all," Mike said. "It might be the other thing."

"That this is deliberate?" Alex looked up at him. "In what way?"

"Well, perhaps it is just a part of the Hole. I know it's not very likely," he added quickly. "But that doesn't mean it can't be true."

"I don't see why it should be," Frankie said.

"Maybe he's just trying to scare us," Geoff said.

"Then he's succeeded," Alex said.

"Oh, come off it."

Alex frowned. "Really. This isn't funny any more. In fact, it never was."

"So we all reckon this is something Martyn intended to happen?" Frankie said.

"I bloody well hope so," Geoff said quietly.

"Why? Do you enjoy this sort of thing?"

Geoff stared at her. "Can't you work it out for yourself?" There was a silence. Everyone waited for him to continue.

"If this is deliberate—if it's Martyn's idea of a good laugh— then everything's going to be all right. Eventually. But if he walked in front of a bus, or dropped off a cliff or something— then we're stuck here, aren't we?" He paused, took a breath. "Like I said. Nobody even knows we're here."

Frankie's mouth was partly open. "That's not what you said before. You said he'd be here any minute."

"Well, it's not looking that way any more, is it?"

"What are you all saying?" Alex asked. "That Martyn's dead? That doesn't seem very likely."

"But we don't know, do we?" Geoff said savagely. He passed a hand across his eyes. "We don't know anything about what's going on up there. The whole fucking world could have ended, for all we know."

"That's just—" Alex began.

"Ridiculous? A bit far-fetched? Sure. But you get the point, don't you? We don't have any control over what goes on out-side. And if Martyn can't get to us, how are we supposed to get out?"

Above them, the blank face of the door sat squarely at the top of the wall, locked shut, forgotten.

. . .

And so I thought I might give it a go . . . just to see what it would be like, to be going out with him. Yes, I was excited; and yes, I thought he was an exciting person to be going out with—sort of slightly dangerous. Like the girl in the sixties movies who falls in with the high-school rebels, and finds they're much more interesting than her prim little friends. It was—I don't know the word for it. Exhilarating, perhaps. Something that had never happened to me before. I was all caught up in it before I knew what I was doing, which was part of the—appeal, that I knew what was going on but didn't stop it. All the time, I was playing games in my mind—trying to find out more about this weird character who was so important to everyone around him.

He—well, I don't know so much about at first, but after a while he did seem to have a pretty strange side to him, which made it all the more real. Things he said, when other people weren't listening, which sounded kind of strange. And sometimes he'd just—stop. Stop what he was doing, whatever he was up to, and freeze there for a while. Sometimes only half a second, although you'd notice it once you were looking . . . sometimes a bit longer. Like something had caught his attention. Like he'd seen something out of the corner of his eye. I think maybe that they were jokes forming in his mind. . . .

It was all icing on the cake, if you know what I mean. Added extras, touches that made this wonderful Martyn character a bit larger than life. That was all he was, to begin with, as well; a character, not really a person. You have to get to know people before you understand them—before you know what they're like, properly. But a character, you can just hear about; hear other people talking and say, Oh yes, I know so-and-so. You don't even have to have met them. Like in newspapers . . .

All the people I knew were pleased for me, which was good as well. I didn't understand much about it all.

So we went out a few times, just like any other couple.

. . .

The afternoon crawled past, and the occupants of the Hole sat and stared at the walls, at the floor, at their feet or belongings, avoiding the others' eyes. There was an ugly tension in the cellar. In the center of the square floor the pile of food was heaped, an insignificant collection of cans and packets, bleakly outlined by their own shadows.

"We could shout for help," Alex said at last. Mike glanced at her quickly, grateful that somebody had spoken. "We could shout together. Maybe someone would hear us."

The others considered. "It's worth a try," Frankie said. "After three, everyone shout Help. One, two, three—"

They shouted. At least, three of them did; Geoff and Liz remained sitting, not moving, not joining in.

"Come on," Alex said irritably. "It might be worth it if you'd make an effort."

"You come on," Geoff returned. "We're underground, for Christ's sake. Who do you think's going to hear us?"

"There might be gardeners, or someone walking past," Frankie said. Geoff sighed.

"OK. Shout all you like. But don't expect me to waste my breath."

"Oh shut up, can't you?" Alex said, with unusual vehemence. "At least we're doing *something*. You aren't. You don't seem to care if we get out or not."

Geoff looked up slowly. "Oh, I care all right," he said. "It would be a bit fucking stupid not to *care*, wouldn't it?" His voice rose in anger. "But what you don't seem to appreciate, what doesn't seem to have penetrated your brain, is that there is nothing we can *do*. Is there?"

The silence, after his words, was hopeless and angry.

"Is there?" he repeated, and this time the words were almost a challenge.

It was Frankie who answered. "Maybe there isn't anything we can do," she said. "Maybe we can't get out. But at least we don't give in." And there was a catch in her voice; Mike, looking at her, saw tears in her eyes.

"Wonderful," Geoff said. "That's all right, then. As long as we don't give in."

Mike ran his knuckle down the edge of his jaw, knowing that Geoff was right, and not wanting to know. Liz, incongruous at the periphery of the exchange, appeared to be reading through past entries in her notebook. Occasionally, he noticed, her eyes flicked to cover the span of the scene in front of her. He wondered what she was thinking; if the cool, quiet Liz was at all scared by what was happening; if, inside, she was beginning to feel a little terrified, as well. Her face gave him no indication; it was completely devoid of expression, like a mask. Her eyes met his for a short moment, and the expressionless expression never altered. As if she'd never seen him.

It was, he realized, a look he'd seen before, but not really recognized: the look you sometimes saw on the faces of people in an examination room, while they scribbled down essays and the white clock on the wall checked off the seconds. Perhaps it was an expression, he conceded; an expression of intense concentration. What was Liz thinking about?

"You don't think that—" Frankie said, and stopped.

"What?"

"Nothing. It doesn't matter."

"Tell me," Alex said. "You don't think that what?"

Frankie hugged her knees against her miserably. "That we might—that nobody might find us, maybe? You don't think that?"

Alex didn't answer. Liz said quietly, "People can live a long time with just water, without any food at all, you know. A very long time."

"And the field trip's due back in a few days," Frankie said.

"Yes. Yes, of course they are." Geoff looked at her with tired contempt.

"How long?" Mike asked Liz.

"I'm not sure. But it's weeks, not days. And we're hardly going to be burning up energy."

"Yeah." Mike frowned. If Liz was so confident, what had she been thinking about so hard?

"Are you sure?" he asked.

"Yes, I'm sure." He saw her look down at her clasped hands, and decided that she was lying.

All the while, we were trying to believe that it wasn't true; that any time now, Martyn would arrive and let us out. It was actually very easy to believe. It was far easier to wait than to try and do anything. As Geoff had said, there was nothing much that we could do.

It was like trying to keep awake when you're incredibly tired; knowing that to close your eyes must mean to sleep, but thinking to yourself that one second won't make any difference, that

two seconds won't either, that ten seconds isn't so much more . . .
and on into unconsciousness. There was too much resistance,
when you tried to think the situation through.

We couldn't climb out. There was only one door, and it was
twelve feet above us. It was locked. The only gap was the keyhole, and we couldn't climb through that. So there was nothing
to do.

What we needed, although we might not have said so at the
time, was a deus ex machina. A hidden trap door. A forgotten
doorway, bricked over but crumbling. A secret passage. A passerby
who happened to hear us talking, and chose to investigate. We
were relying on a god, of sorts, to get us out. Not Martyn. He
was never a god, although perhaps he was a step nearer one than
we were.

We sat and waited, and thereby helped on Martyn's plan.

EIGHT

Nobody wanted to be the first to eat. They sat, as the day wore on, with taut hunger crawling inside them, unwilling to say anything about it. The door did not open; there was no sound from the world above. It was as if the cellar was all that existed. When evening came, they turned off the light and settled to sleep.

Mike lay awake for a long time in the pitch blackness of the Hole, running over and over in his mind the possibilities that faced them. He knew that the others were probably doing the same thing; he wondered if, by thinking about it, he could accomplish anything. The best thing to do would be to sleep, until someone discovered them. Sleep, and forget that it was all happening; and conserve your strength for whatever might lie ahead.

It was relatively early evening, and the sun in the world above would still be shining as the dregs of the day bled off towards dusk. He looked for the star, and found it; it was dim, and just before Mike finally drifted into sleep, it seemed that the star winked once, as if at some private joke.

I can remember that night with a vivid clarity born of terror. I had no idea what to do, and I could not believe that I had become involved with the Hole to the extent that there was nothing I could do about it. Always, in the past, I had been the one accountable for my actions; had had to be constantly sensible and cautious, had had to think ahead and take care of myself. And here I was, the victim of something that was so senseless that I should have seen through it at a glance. I was unable to forgive myself for that; I would have thought myself the last person to be swept up by charisma above and beyond common sense. But that was what had happened. And when I look back, and consider that the entire school had been swept up with Martyn along with me, I can perhaps partly understand what had happened. Understand, but still not forgive.

There are few worse things than being at the mercy of your own lack of vision. The more I examined our situation, that night, the more starkly apparent it became that the Hole had been engineered with uncanny precision; that there was no flaw in Martyn's plan at all, and that we were completely entangled and ensnared. It was bleak, and—even for someone who had been used to spending much time with herself—I was also very alone.

Mike's troubled sleep was finally broken at some time in the early morning. For a short while he could almost have imagined himself somewhere else, outside the Hole and away from the nightmare that it was becoming. But the hard floor of the cellar, and the uncompromising darkness that blocked up his eyes, forced down on him the reality of where he was and what was happening. Quietly, for fear of disturbing the others, he got up and crept across the room, through the doorway and around into the lavatory. With the cold porcelain rim against his knees he peed.

"Mike?"

The shock of the whisper made him jump. Hastily hitching up his boxer shorts, he turned. The short hallway was still deep in darkness. "Who's that?"

"It's me." A pause. "Liz. Sorry."

"Christ. You shouldn't do that."

"Mm. Don't flush that, will you?"

"No," he agreed, keeping his voice down. "Did I wake you?"

"Not really. I've been doing a lot of thinking."

"I thought you had."

There was a click, and Liz's pocket flashlight flooded a patch of yellow light onto the floor. Her hair was an unruly tumble across the shoulders of her pyjamas, and she looked tired. Mike saw that she was carrying the empty lemonade bottle in her other hand, and restrained a strong impulse to laugh. "What were you going to do with that?" he asked. "Surely not a midnight feast?"

"Look, can we go through here? I don't want to wake anyone, but I want to talk to you." She pointed the flashlight at the small empty room across from the lavatory.

"OK." Mike followed her through and they sat down, rather awkwardly, facing each other.

"This thing's nearly dead. I wish I'd brought some new batteries." Liz put the flashlight down on the floor, and a delta of dim light made long ravines of the cracks between the flags. "But then, there are a lot of things I wish I'd brought."

Mike nodded. "What do you think's going to happen?" he asked.

"I was hoping you might tell me," she said. "Geoff's beginning to realize what's going on, and I think Frankie's halfway there. But Geoff's already given up, I think; and Frankie—" She hesitated. "Frankie's not really much good for anything."

"What is going on?" Mike asked, almost against his will. He didn't want to hear the answer, he realized. Liz smiled, a strange smile with no mirth in it.

"That depends. I know what I think the next stage is, but I'm not . . . I'm not completely sure yet. We're about to find out, though."

"How?"

"In a minute. You haven't told me yet . . . what you think this is all about."

"I think it's gone wrong," Mike said. "Hideously wrong. I keep trying to see a way round it, or out of it, but there isn't one. It's terrifying."

Liz looked at him in silence. At last she said, "Yes. It is terrifying. But I don't think it's gone wrong at all. And that's the scariest part."

"So you think that this is still part of a stupid joke?"

The smile again. "No. Hardly." Then, after a pause, "Mike—I'm really scared."

"So am I," he said quietly; and realized, at the same time, that he was.

The light from the flashlight faded abruptly, and then juddered back to its original strength. Liz glanced at it, and shook her head as if her concentration had been broken.

"Come on, then," she said. "I suppose we'd better find out if I'm right."

Mystified, Mike followed as she made her way back to the lavatory. Kneeling by the tap, where it projected from the stonework, Liz set the lemonade bottle on the ground.

"Hold this, could you?" she said, handing Mike the flashlight. "And shine it so that I can see. Shit. I wish I'd brought new batteries. I think we'll need them."

Mike stared as she balanced the neck of the plastic bottle under the spout of the tap. "Two liters," she murmured to herself, and slowly turned the tap on. A trickle of water snaked silently down the inside of the bottle, and then, as she gently increased the flow, there was a faint hissing from the tap. Mike watched the water rise inside the bottle—a third of the way, halfway. There was a sudden, noisy spluttering and a brief spray of water jetted out onto his feet. Liz didn't move. The water was past halfway, almost coming up above the wide green label, when there was another gushing splutter, and the steady trickle died to nothing. Still very slowly, Liz opened the tap all the way.

"That's it," she said. "No more water."

"It's run out?" Mike said, in an aghast whisper.

"It's been turned off," she corrected, and screwed the top of the lemonade bottle firmly back into place. "You still don't really get it, do you?"

"What?" he said, and the word came out as if from a distance, because he already knew. They went back to the room opposite.

Liz said, "I saw this coming this afternoon. It was something I said myself that made me think of it."

"That we could manage a long time without food," Mike said, remembering.

"Right. But not so long without water ... and I thought, if Martyn really is doing this, if he's really in charge still, then that will be the next thing to go."

"And it has," Mike said. "This—" He struggled for the right words. "This is unbelievable. It's insane."

"Martyn's insane," Liz said.

"I know. No one in their right minds would pull a stunt like this."

"I mean it," she said. Mike looked at her. "Martyn's not just pulling a stunt. That's pretty obvious, isn't it? We're not expected to walk out of this. This isn't the work of a sane mind, Mike."

Mike rested his head in his hands. "So what the hell are we supposed to do?" he asked. "The bastard's one step ahead of us all the way. We've got nothing to fight back with."

"Well," Liz said. "Maybe. But I'm getting closer...." She stopped. "We've got to track down what he thinks is going to happen. If we can—get inside Martyn, be Martyn, we might find a way around this."

"Do you really think so?"

"No. Not really." She sighed, and for a moment, with her chin on her knees, she looked very young and afraid. "But at least I'm beginning to understand ... I was ahead of him on the water, at least."

"But we haven't got time to play games," Mike said. "What do we have? About a liter of water. How long will that last five of us?"

"No. More than that."

"Not much more," Mike said, looking dubiously at the bottle.

"In the cistern, I mean," Liz said. "There's got to be quite a bit in there. I wonder if he's remembered that?"

Mike realized just how little thought he had been giving the situation. Liz, sitting there quietly all afternoon, had already managed to predict the next phase of the Hole, and was thinking her way around it. With a hideous shiver, he saw how easy it would have been, without even hesitating, to flush the lavatory and lose what little water they had left.

"Why are you telling me all this?" he asked.

"I don't know. It seems right, somehow. . . . Maybe because we both saw the keyhole together. At least we're thinking in that direction."

"The keyhole winked at me, I swear it," Mike said, and giggled.

"What?"

"Just before I went to sleep. I saw it wink."

"Don't go crazy on me," Liz warned.

"What do we tell the others?" he asked, and was ashamed at having to ask the question.

"We'll have to tell them about the water, of course," Liz said. "But if it's all the same with you, I'd rather say that there must be a tank somewhere that's run out, rather than suggesting that it's been turned off. Say that Martyn probably budgeted for three days. We'll need to get whatever's in the cistern into bottles and things. Geoff's got a lot."

"Do you think they'll believe it?"

"Geoff won't. Frankie and Alex might, I suppose." She

blew a strand of hair away from her face. "We'll just have to be convincing."

"Right," Mike said hollowly.

It was early in the day, but I put down the pen I had been using and pushed my chair away from the table. The front door, far below, swung shut, and I could hear voices at the foot of the stairs.

"Mike?"

It wasn't him. I turned back to the attic room, disappointed. I could have done with someone else at that point, someone who'd been there. I had known before I began that this would not be easy, but that didn't change the fact that, the more I wrote, the more aware I became of my own insignificance. Not at all easy. A friendly face would have helped.

I sat down again, moved the pen in idle circles, stared out of the window at the blackbirds and the trees, trying to avoid the things that had to be written out.

When the next day began, they told the others and filled the remaining bottles with water from the cistern in the lavatory. For a time, Mike had wondered if perhaps the feed pipes to the cistern might still be working. They were not; a little extra leaked out from the ballcock, but not much. The atmosphere had immediately become far more tense than before; the others, on hearing about the water, accepted the notion of the tank easily enough; but still there was a pervading sense of something that was coming close to being panic.

"I'm hungry," Alex said quietly, when they'd finished. "What do we do? Eat now or save it until later?"

"We save it," Liz said. "As long as possible."

To Mike's eyes, the remaining food looked totally inadequate. It was hardly enough for a snack, let alone a meal for five. The collection of water bottles, ranked up against the wall, seemed slightly more reassuring. He kept reminding himself that they had at least kept ahead on that score.

"We'll have to make sure that we eat and drink as little as possible," Frankie said. "And make sure that everything's shared equally."

Liz looked up from her notebook. "It's not quite that simple," she said.

"Why not?"

"I want to see those packages, and work out what food we have in terms of nutrients. I think I can do that. Does anyone here do biology?"

Nobody did.

"That's a shame," Liz said mildly. "There's something really important about salts and water, and keeping the two balanced. But I don't know enough to tell which way to adjust our diet. We shouldn't eat salty foods, I think."

"Brilliant," Geoff said. "You *think*. So we might end up poisoned or dead of dehydration because you can't quite remember what to eat and what not to eat."

Liz turned back to her notebook without answering. After a minute or two, Frankie silently gathered together the remaining food and took it over to where Liz was sitting.

"Here you go," she said. And then, "I wish I hadn't eaten all that Turkish delight. That's got sugar in, hasn't it? It could have been important."

"Don't worry about it." She smiled briefly. "At least we're all healthy enough."

"I don't see what you're playing at," Geoff said. "You don't know what you're doing. You said that yourself. Why should we trust you to get it right?"

"I'm just trying to make sure that everyone gets what they need," Liz said. "I'm doing the best I can. Sure, I wish we had a scientist here; it would make life a lot easier. But since we don't, you'll have to make do with me."

"What do you mean, you're making sure that everyone gets what they need?" Geoff said. "It's simple. Everyone gets a fair share. There's no more to it."

"A fair share's not the same as an equal share," Liz said. For the first time in the conversation, she looked up and her eyes met Geoff's. "I hope that's all right."

There was a pause. Liz and Geoff remained unmoving, looking steadily at each other. Then Geoff turned away, and it was Frankie who spoke next.

"I'm pleased that someone's doing something," she said. "I don't care how much food you give me. Liz knows more than the rest of us, and I think she's sorting things out really well." She laughed. "We'll probably be out of here in no time."

"As if anyone gave a fuck what you think," Geoff said quietly. Frankie drew breath to answer, and then stopped; a look of confusion crossed her face, and she said, "Liz? We will get out, won't we?"

"Of course we will," Liz said.

"I knew we would." Frankie turned over onto her side, so that she was facing away from the group; but even Mike could see she was crying.

Martyn was nothing if not careful. I can remember the preparations for a number of his jokes, and the one thing that strikes me—in each instance—as strange is that we only realized exactly what was happening *afterwards*. While the thing was in progress it was funny; before it took place it seemed half hilarious and half childish. But afterwards, when the mirth could be swept away and one or two of us could see the true face of the joke, things were always unexpected. Gibbon left, later that term, and didn't come back; some of the others changed dramatically, as well. It was an aftermath that was, itself, more devastating than the incident.

It still seems unforgivably foolish that I could ever allow a person like Martyn to have such complete, unalloyed control over my life. But none of us imagined what the Hole might be; simply because the concept was too awful to be entertained even as a passing thought. And too unbelievable. You don't examine every inch of a prank suggested by the school wit to see if it's going to cost you your life; there's no need.

If only we had, for some strange reason, done just that. If only one of us—for any reason—had decided not to do the Hole, the entire fabric of the thing would have been rendered useless to Martyn. Someone on the outside would know, and that would make it far too dangerous for him. If only we had told anyone where we were going. But, of course, we had not; and we had congratulated ourselves on having become involved in something that would no doubt become one of the many legends that Our Glorious School collected.

I have in front of me the cardboard box. There are nine cassettes on the top, held in two bundles by elastic bands. Seven of them are marked LISA in my own handwriting; black pen on the inlay card. The conversations recorded on them go a little way towards showing another side of Martyn, one which we had never glimpsed at school. If Lisa and I had talked back then, before the Hole, I would never have allowed Martyn to use me the way he did; to use us all. The other two tapes, in the separate bundle, are not marked. There must have been many more of them, of course; but those have gone, and we'll never know where. Besides, there's nothing on them that I don't know already. Perhaps, with the others in that series, we could have convinced someone about what really happened, shown someone what Martyn was. But at the end, Martyn managed to keep just one step ahead of us.

NINE

By midday, Mike found himself faint with hunger. The gnawing stomach pains that had come the previous evening were supplemented by a terrible thirst that he was unable to ignore. It was lunchtime; he couldn't shake off the thought that it was lunchtime, and that they should be eating and drinking. He hadn't said anything, of course. He had promised himself that he wouldn't be the first one to mention food.

It was Liz who did it for all of them.

"We'd better eat something," she said. "Not much." They divided out tiny portions of the remaining food—dry pasta, a little canned meat. Some water in a cup. How much water was it that you had to drink each day? Something like four pints, Mike thought. One small cupful was all they allowed themselves. With unusual foresight, Mike wondered who would be the first to question the allocated portions, to demand more for some reason or other. It would have to happen eventually. But it would not be him.

If anything, eating the tiny amount available had increased his awareness of hunger. It was ironic: to eat entailed a heightened reminder of the need to eat. He smiled at the tricks his body was playing on him, but there wasn't much comfort in the joke.

"When we get out, we can all go to a restaurant somewhere," Frankie said. "I want something really heavy . . . a steak and kidney pie, I think."

"Don't," Alex said.

"Oh. I'm sorry," Frankie said. Mike didn't think she looked sorry. The expression on Frankie's face was a difficult one to judge. "I just like food so much, it's strange not to have enough." She smiled to herself. "At home we have a freezer full of stuff."

"Shut up," Geoff said. "Eat the shit you've been given and shut up."

Frankie looked at her handful and shrugged. "OK."

It seemed a long time to go until the evening. Mike wished he could think of a way to get through those hours safely. He wished he knew what Liz was thinking.

"At least there isn't anything more that can go wrong," he said, trying to sound cheerful.

"As if this isn't enough for you," Geoff said. "I can't believe it. You're telling us to look on the bright side of this?" He drained his plastic cup of water and abruptly crushed it, letting it drop by his side. "There isn't much of a bright side to look on. We're going to die, you realize? Yes? So don't give me any crap about nothing much more going wrong."

"There are a few things that could go wrong yet," Liz said, but nobody was listening.

"I think we'll get out," Mike said, angrily. He was angry with Geoff for making things worse, for emphasizing the hopelessness that he had been trying to forget.

"No you don't," Geoff contradicted sharply. "You're conning yourself. Inside you know the truth just as much as I do. Or her—" pointing at Frankie—"or Liz or Alex. You all know, really. You're just too fucking stupid to face up to it."

Mike didn't know what to say. And then Liz spoke, and her voice was so cold that Mike hardly recognized it.

"Do you call what you're doing facing up to it?" she asked. "I'm really impressed. If facing up to it entails snivelling like a spoiled child every time anyone else says anything, you're welcome to it."

Geoff's mouth hung slightly open. There was a dull anger in his eyes that didn't quite surface.

"Fuck you," he said lamely. Mike swallowed, but Liz didn't answer.

I didn't see very much of him for a while—at the beginning of the holidays, that is. It wasn't much of a surprise. Besides, I had things to do myself: the beginning of the serious A-level work. Nobody takes the first year too seriously, but you know . . . so when the Easter holiday came, I didn't mind not seeing Martyn. There was nothing strange about it, I mean.

I never knew anything about the Hole. He never said anything, he didn't let on in any way. I went round to his house once or twice, and everything was the same as it had always been . . . there wasn't anything different. . . . If I had known, I would have done something. Really. But he hadn't let anyone know anything—it's pretty obvious why, I suppose. I can't believe that it was all going on, and I was doing all the usual things, completely—not knowing a thing about it. But there was nothing, not even a clue in the way he behaved or anything. There was nothing at all.

Really, I wanted it to end, the thing with Martyn—I mean, the novelty wore off pretty quick, and I was left—attached, I suppose, to this guy who I didn't really know and wasn't even sure I liked all that much. I'd thought he was wonderful to begin with, but like I said. . . . Things were a lot different back then. Perhaps I liked him more than I think now. Maybe. But I do know that I wasn't keen on this dragging on, or anything. I was hoping to talk to him about it some time, but he wasn't around all that much.

I shut the machine off, and sat back. He had been astonishing, the way that he had carried on completely normally, while all the time knowing what he knew. Since it happened, there has never been any doubt in my mind that Martyn was anything less than totally insane. His was an organized, not a chaotic insanity, which made it all the more difficult to identify. The term "psychopath" goes less than halfway towards describing Martyn. He was brilliant: a dangerous madman with a genius for invention and incredible charisma. He was also a madman who knew enough to conceal his own madness; which brings me to Martyn's childhood. About *that* I know nothing. Joining Our Glorious School at sixth-form level, he might just as well have stepped out of a tear in the sky. His aunt and uncle owned a house some miles away from the village, where he lived; but beyond those meager details, there is nothing.

What can he have been like as a child? What had happened to him, to make him what he was? If only we had the answers, I keep thinking. Maybe we could do something to stop others like him. I don't know.

Thinking about Martyn makes everything else seem as thin as paper. And even though I cannot imagine what was inside his head—and I've tried—I sometimes find myself realizing how similar, despite all our differences, we are. To the extent that, if there was no chance of discovery, if I could be guaranteed anonymity in the deed, I would not hesitate to kill Martyn. I mean that. It's a completely theoretical point, of course; I have far too much trust in forensic science, and far too little in my own ingenuity, to try my hand at killing people. But I've certainly thought about it. I wonder if anyone would try to dispute that the world would be a better place without Martyn in it? I know four other people who would not.

That afternoon, which seemed like an age, began the final tearing-down of walls. Only the fact that I was still too desperate to give up kept me from starting to lose my mind.

"Christ, I'm hungry," Alex said. "How long until we eat again?"

Liz looked at her watch. "Eat at six. That's another hour and a half. Then try to get some sleep."

"An early night?" Frankie asked.

"Yes. Keep your strength up."

Mike lay on his side, with his arms wrapped around his belly. He could hear the voices, but they didn't affect him; the words weren't important. He was looking at the canvas flap of his knapsack. Somewhere in there, he remembered putting a bag of chips. Tube-shaped chips in a blue bag. He couldn't look now, of course, because the others would see. But if he waited until nighttime, he could eat them in the dark, and no one would know. He grinned; they'd completely slipped his mind. He could imagine the taste of them right there.

"I'm really hungry now, Liz," Alex said. "Badly. I don't feel good."

"None of us feels good," Liz reminded her. "Personally, I feel like shit."

Alex smiled feebly. "Yeah. Know what you mean."

"I think an early night's a good idea," Frankie said. "We need to keep our strength up for tomorrow."

"That's right," Geoff said. "What are you going to do, Frankie? Climb out?"

"You're so thick, sometimes," she told him.

Alex shivered, and then clenched her fists. "Ow," she said, and whatever pain had gripped her made her grimace. "That doesn't feel too good at all."

"Is it cramps?" Liz asked.

Alex nodded miserably. "I think so. Ah, shit. That's not good. That's not at all good." She blinked, and stumbled to her feet. "I feel sick," she said, and broke into a clumsy half-run for the lavatory. Liz, looking to Mike's eyes infinitely weary, got up and followed her.

After a moment, there was a hollow sound of retching. Mike could hear Liz's voice, "Wipe your mouth. OK, OK." There was a pause, and Alex coughed, a staccato sound that was followed immediately by more vomiting. Mike winced. There must be hardly anything to bring up, he thought; and none of it was exactly spare. It was fairly easy to divorce himself from his own hunger enough to feel sorry for Alex.

Geoff sat up. "That's it," he said. "If that's what this fucking diet does to people, I'm eating now."

"No!" Frankie shouted, as Geoff picked up one of the opened cans of meat. "You can't do that!"

"Stop me, then," he said, with no inflection at all. Using his fingers, he dug a chunk of the stuff out of the can and swallowed it.

"What do you think you're doing?" Everybody turned, to see Liz in the doorway. Holding on to her shoulder was Alex, who was shaking visibly. Mike noticed with disgust that there was a thick string of vomit down the side of her chin. Geoff stopped, his hand halfway from his mouth.

"Killer," Liz said flatly.

Geoff stared at her, the small lumps and smears of canned meat on his hand glistening. "What did you say?"

"You," she replied. "That's what you are, if you eat that. You think you need it more than anyone else?" She stepped forward, leaving Alex holding the door jamb. "OK. Who's going to go without so you can eat? Pick someone." There was a long silence.

"Pick someone, I said." Liz moved closer still, and her fierce eyes burned up at Geoff's. "Frankie? You don't give a shit about her. Why not let her die? You could have twice as much then. Or Alex. Doesn't look very well, does she? Maybe she won't last much longer. Maybe it's not worth wasting food on her. Mike? Didn't you always complain that he'd eaten too much? You could pay him back now. Let him starve, rather than you. Or me. Why not? I'm smaller than you, so there's not much I could do about it. And I don't think you like me all that much right now, so it wouldn't be too difficult, would it? Go on. Pick someone." Ridiculously, she pushed him in the chest with the flat of her hand, and Geoff took a quick step backwards.

"Pick someone now, or start acting like a human being."

She turned away, and went back to Alex. "There's some toilet paper here," Mike heard her say as she turned the corner. "Let's get you cleaned up."

Geoff stood there, and for the first time in quite a while Mike saw real emotions in his face. It had seemed up to then that the Hole had leached any feeling out of Geoff, but as Mike watched, Geoff put the can back where it had been and sat down on his sleeping bag. After a long time, he looked up.

"I'm sorry," he said quietly.

"That's OK," Mike told him, aware that it wasn't—not really—but intensely relieved that Liz's gambit had worked. It wasn't until much later that he began to realize just how important and effective her words had been: She had laid out, in plain view, some of the thoughts that were eventually to cross all their minds, and had defused them. It was a public act that was not just for Geoff's benefit. But at that point, in his innocence, Mike could not conceive that he would ever be able to harbor such thoughts about someone else.

It was somewhere in the middle of it all that I began to see what I'd been missing that far. Gradually, an idea began to take shape. It wasn't much, but it was an idea. And, surprisingly, there was a simple way to find out whether I was right or not. But it involved waiting. It would take time. And we were running far too short on that.

• • •

The sound of laughter, and the shouts of children playing at the water's edge, danced in the thick afternoon air. We sat, Mike and I, with the water curling around our ankles.

"When are you going to take me to America?" I asked.

"Sometime soon. Let's earn some money first, all right?"

"You earn the money. I'll just lie back and let it all happen."

"That's what you think, is it?" He waved a dripping foot over my leg.

"Hey! Stop it!"

"You should get off your butt and find a job," he said.

"No way. I'm having far too good a time. Except for the writing, and so on."

"Don't you enjoy it?" He thought. "I don't suppose you do."

"No. But it's already beginning to feel like I'm losing part of it . . . as if the more I write down, the further away from it I get. It's only when I'm actually in there, and it all comes to the surface, that it's not so good."

"Ah. Yes." We sat and splashed water like children.

"So," Mike said. "Where have you got up to?"

"The important part," I told him. "You can read it once it's done."

"OK."

"I love you."

"I love you, too. Respectfully," he added. "I love you for your brilliant mind."

"Bullshit," I said in mock outrage.

"All right, all right, I admit it. I just lust after your body."

"That's better."

"Good." He sighed. "Come on. I'll walk you home."

"So soon?"

"I've got to go into the village before the shops close."

"I'll come," I said.

"You will not."

"Oh? How come?"

"Something to do with someone who claims to have a birthday soon and who would probably not be very happy if they didn't get something or other from this other person they just happen to know," he said, and grinned. "I've got to sort it all out."

"Ah," I said, and felt warm inside. "That's OK, then."

"So I should hope. Dry your feet, woman."

The woods were charged with life and heat as we walked the footpath towards the village.

"Have a drink," Liz said. "You need it."

Alex shook her head. "I'd better not," she said. "I might just bring it up again. Besides, we need it."

"Nobody needs it more than you do," Liz said firmly. "If you keep going without water, you'll end up seeing things crawling out of the walls." She poured half a cup from the lemonade bottle. "Sip it slowly," she added.

Alex did so. "What's wrong with me?" she said, almost to herself. "I feel so ill."

"It'll get worse," Liz told her. Mike thought it was an unnecessarily harsh thing to have said, but strangely enough Alex didn't appear to take it that way.

"I suppose so," she said.

"You're going to have to force yourself to keep things down," Liz said. "Shit. I wish we'd got some of that powder that you mix up and drink. The stuff that keeps you going for months." She smiled at herself. "And a lot of other things, as well."

Mike felt his stomach twist in anger as he watched Alex drinking. The water looked cool and pure. He could have drunk gallons of it.

"What do we do about—about the mess?" Alex asked, in a small voice.

"Not much we can do. Don't worry." Liz sighed. "It's going to be foul in any case, I'm afraid."

Mike, working out that she meant the lavatory now that they'd emptied the cistern, grimaced in disgust.

"Isn't it time for some food?" Frankie asked. Mike frowned. There was something strange about her voice that he couldn't quite put his finger on.

"Yes. Everyone have something," Liz said, and once again they went through the slow ritual of dividing out portions of food. Mike stuffed his handful of meat and biscuit into his mouth as quickly as possible, having to fight back a strong urge to gag. The two inches of water in the cup washed his throat clear and left him desperate for the next mouthful. There was nothing else. He swallowed. The action hurt, in a way that made him think of tonsillitis as a child. He'd had his tonsils taken out years ago, so it couldn't be that.

"That was nice," Frankie said. "Not very much of it, but that's OK. There's not so long to go now, is there?"

"I don't think so," Liz said automatically. She was forcing one finger into a crack in the floor. Her hair, beginning to look matted and greasy, hung in a heavy swatch over one eye. She looked up at the others, and smiled. "You guys look glum," she said. "Cheer up. I know it's a bitch, but we will make it, really. We've got food and water and light, and we've got each others' company. Christ, it's almost cozy, like Alex said."

Alex's mouth twisted into a small grin. "I still feel bad," she said.

"Yeah. Have a little more to drink. Not much." Liz poured some more water. "There. Slowly, remember."

"I can't wait to get out of here," Frankie said. "I'm going to find Martyn and pull his balls off."

"I'll help," Mike said, and his voice sounded faint and wrong in his head. He looked at Liz, and her clear eyes stared back at him. Astonishingly, he could have sworn that they were laughing at him.

And so we get closer and closer. Desperation kept me going, but all around people were falling apart, just caving in as if there was nothing in their centers except stale air. Frankie was right. But it was going to be me who pulled Martyn's balls off, if you like; and I was going to do it from right there. If only. If it would work. I'd done everything possible, without making it obvious. . . . The idea burned in my head like a brand. I couldn't even imagine that it might go wrong, because if it did we would all be dead. And nobody can really imagine that, can they?

And so I fostered and nurtured it, waiting all along for a sign that the time was right. The clues had been there all along.

That night, when we switched off the light and tried to settle down, I allowed myself a tiny smile of hope. It had to work. There was no alternative.

But even though I had all that certainty to wad up around me as a wall against the night, I still felt very small, and very afraid, and very alone.

TEN

After the breathing of those around him had died away to a murmur, Mike slowly raised himself up on one elbow. The flap of his knapsack was unbuckled, and he slipped his hand inside, feeling for the plastic bag that he knew was there. The wait, while the others tossed and turned, and muttered, and rolled over, had seemed endless. But he was sure that he was safe now.

Stupidly, he couldn't find the bag. More impatiently, with less care, he felt around the inside of the knapsack once again. Some shirts he'd already worn; nothing more. Where was it? A burning anger rose within him, and he began to search a third time. Had it dropped out? Had someone taken it?

Then the memory came back to him, and his fists clenched tightly. He had given the chips to Geoff, early on, probably the first night. For a long time he lay there, uncomfortably propped up on one elbow, staring into the darkness and cursing himself silently. He had got through the afternoon by promising himself those hidden, forgotten chips; by imagining how they would taste, what they would feel like in his mouth. What a stupid mistake.

He felt a gentle brush of movement against his arm, and froze.

"Who's that?"

"Me. Liz," she whispered. "I need to talk to you. Can you make it to the room round the corner, without waking anyone up?"

"Yes, I think so."

"I'll follow in a bit."

Mike made his way gropingly to the doorway, and then felt along the short passage, running his fingertips along the walls. After a short time, he heard Liz following him. They sat down in darkness.

"This is getting to be a habit," Mike whispered.

"I thought you would be asleep," she whispered back. "I was afraid I'd have to wake you. What were you doing?"

"I thought I had some food left. I was going to eat it when everyone was asleep. Shit." He rubbed a hand over his eyes, which felt hot and gritty. Swirls of color appeared in the darkness around him. "I know what it sounds like, but that—the thought of it was all that kept me going. And it's not there."

"Ah."

"I feel really terrible about it. But I feel hungry, too. And thirsty."

"Don't be guilty," Liz said. "It's perfectly natural. I bet everyone's done something similar."

"I bet you haven't," Mike said dismally. "You're too perfect."

"I went one better," Liz said. "Here." She caught his arm, and handed him something. A bottle.

"What's this?"

"Water. Drink half. The others don't know about it, so don't worry."

Mike drank, greedily, and had to force himself to break off before the bottle was empty. "Shit. That's amazing. I can smell it. It's wonderful. Where did you get this?"

"I kept it all along," Liz said casually. "Can I have it back? I'd rather like some as well."

"Oh. Yes." Mike passed it back, and doing so was agony.

"That's better," Liz murmured, after drinking.

"How come you shared it with me?" Mike asked.

"What?"

"Really. If I'd had those chips, I don't suppose ... no, I know I wouldn't have let anyone else have any. Thanks."

"It's OK. Besides, we're friends, right?"

"We are?"

"I think so."

"Good," Mike said. "I think so, too."

"I think we're all going to need friends," Liz said thoughtfully. "It's not over yet."

"Is it ever going to be over?" Mike asked. "I've been thinking. We aren't going to get out; Martyn's never going to come and open the door. And that means we're going to die."

"I know. Maybe. But—I keep on finding out more, all the time. I think I've discovered something really important. You helped, too."

"What?"

"Remember when we found out about the water?"

"Yes. Too well."

"OK. And I said I knew it was going to be the next stage, because something I'd said had suggested the idea to me?"

"Yeah. I've got a strong feeling of déjà vu," Mike said.

"Bear with me, OK? I've been thinking about all that. Doesn't it seem strange to you that one minute I mention that we can go for ages with no food, and the next minute the water stops?"

"If that was the next thing he was going to do, it doesn't matter whether you worked it out beforehand or not," Mike said. "It would have happened in any case."

"Hm," Liz said. "That's exactly what I've been puzzling over. And then you said something . . . you said that the keyhole winked at you. I was hardly listening at the time, but that was a pretty strange thing to say. What did you see?"

Mike shuffled his feet, embarrassed. "I was half asleep," he said. "It was nothing, really."

"What did you see?" she persisted.

"Just—it sounds stupid. It just looked as if the star went out and then came on again. Like an eye winking."

"As if for just a moment it had been blocked off?"

"I suppose so."

"As if someone had walked past the door?"

Mike sat in silence, his mind suddenly a confused turmoil of ideas and inferences. "Yes. It could have been. But what—"

"Listen to me. It was Martyn, I think. No. I'm pretty sure it was."

"My God," Mike said, weakly. "He's some kind of monster. What's he doing, walking around here?"

"That's it," Liz said. "That's what I worked out. I mention—indirectly, sure—that the water's good news, and the water is cut off. Cause and effect."

"What are you saying?" Mike, trying to keep up with the conversation, could almost see Liz's face in the darkness, a small, excited smile on her lips.

"He can hear us, Mikey. That's it. It has to be that he can hear us."

"Now?" Mike whispered, aghast.

"I don't think so. Just the main room."

"You mean he's got his ear to the door?" Mike said.

"Don't be thick," Liz said absently. "Of course he hasn't. He's got to be out there in the big wide world, making sure that he's still in full view. But think about this: He's set up the Hole, this incredible creation that's his own work. Do you think he could put up with not knowing what's going on inside? I don't think so. He'd want to know who cracks up first, know whether anybody kills someone before it's over, know who lasts longest and why. He's not going to just abandon us. We're too important."

"And he can hear us?"

Liz took a breath. "I think the main room is—whatever the term is. Wired. Bugged. That he can record what's going on in there. What you saw—the winking keyhole—was someone coming to pick up the lastest recording. Martyn, I'd guess. I don't think he would let anyone else in on this, do you?"

"No," Mike said. He felt stunned. "You worked all this out?"

"I can test it, too," Liz said. "I set that up today. So we'll know, soon enough, whether I'm right, or whether I'm just crazy and you're hallucinating."

"OK," Mike said. "What's the test?"

"I'm counting on the fact that Martyn's annoyed with me," she said. "If you look at things from his point of view, I've screwed it up for him. Possibly. Or maybe he thinks I'm interesting. Either way, the business with the water and the bottles will have got his attention. And today I made some comment or other about how we should be thankful that we've still got food and water and light. If he picks up on that, what's the next thing we lose?"

"Light," Mike said.

"Exactly. That's what I think, too. So if he really is listening, I reckon the lights will go out some time tomorrow."

"That's not going to be nice," Mike said dubiously.

"I'm not keen on it either. But it won't kill us, and we'll at least know that he's there if it happens."

"What do we do then? Do we—try and bargain, or beg to be let out?"

There was a pause. Liz said, "Do you think that would work?"

Mike thought it over. "No," he said eventually. "Not with Martyn."

"I don't think so either. No. We'll have to wait and see . . . and if he really is listening, we'll take it from there."

"You'll think about it?" Mike asked.

"Of course I will. You, too."

"OK," he said.

"There has to be a way out," Liz said, almost to herself. "I know there has to be."

• • •

I sat, holding the cassette tightly. It would be so easy to take it—a small plastic box—and burn it, or crush it. It would be so easy to get rid of. But that wouldn't erase the story on it, because the story happened to real people.

Silently, I put the cassette back with the rest. The time for that isn't just yet. Deep within me, the temptation is to stop now, at this place, because the worst parts follow on from here. But so do the best parts, and the story has to be told out.

Mike's night was long, and sleep came with difficulty. Dreams and nightmares clawed at him, and at times he couldn't differentiate between the two: whether a dream of escape, of stepping out into the sunlight and fresh air, was not, in fact, a nightmare. Part of him hated Liz for awakening even a frail hope when he had just begun to come to terms with the idea of dying. It was a thought which he could not ever remember having entertained; an impossible thought for someone his age. And now it was days away, not decades. Once or twice, in the night, voices whispered that were not the voices of those in the Hole. It was almost more than he could cope with. He didn't want this darkness to last all day, as well, but ironically he also did want the lights to go out; because if Liz was right, then just perhaps there might be a way out.

Day came. Mike was awake, and had been for what felt like an age. The star, far above him, glowed feebly, tiredly, but steadily.

The others crawled their way back to wakefulness, and Geoff turned on the light. Mike, almost expecting that it would not work, was dazzled by its flare. He looked at once at Liz, and the bulb was reflected in the deepening hollows of her eyes.

Mike surveyed his companions with something approaching compassion. Their faces were stark, gray. A scattering of hard-looking pimples had broken out across Alex's forehead. Geoff's normally strong frame was slouched in the corner of two walls. They seemed like a cruel parody of down-and-outs, street children. He wondered how long they would be able to last if— if there wasn't a way out. The line of bottles against the wall looked good, until you counted how many were full. Under a third. For one person, maybe it would constitute some degree of hope. But for five?

"I want to do my teeth," Frankie said. "My mouth feels nasty."

"You can't," Alex said. "Not enough water."

"I need a crap," Geoff said, standing up.

"When do we get out?" Frankie asked. "Liz? When do we get out?"

Liz didn't answer.

"Do you remember all that?" I asked.

"Yes. Too clearly." He smiled. "You frightened me, you know."

"I know. I frightened me, too. It was all part of it."

"Sometimes, in a way, you still do."

I was confused. "What way?"

"Well ... just that I see you here as an ordinary person. Everybody does. But that's not quite right, is it? I saw a different side to you, down there."

"We all met different sides of ourselves," I agreed. "Be grateful to Martyn for that, if you like."

"I don't think so," he grinned. "I don't think I'm grateful to Martyn for anything much."

"You realize something?"

"What?"

"We wouldn't be sitting here if it wasn't for Martyn. We'd just have walked off in different directions."

"Maybe not," he protested. "I mean, we might have got together at school in any case."

"Oh, I don't think so," I smiled back. "She was far too strange and standoffish."

"And he was far too immature and silly."

"Right." I laughed with him. "So we've got Martyn to thank for that, at least."

"Gee, thanks, Martyn."

"Watch it," I warned. "I'm completely unpredictable."

"I love it," he said.

It happened about midday.

"When do we eat?" Alex said.

"How do you feel?" Mike asked her.

"Better, I think. I feel—like there's nothing inside me at all. Well, there isn't, I suppose." She smiled weakly. "I don't seem to care much any more."

"Here," Liz said. "Have some food." She was halfway across the floor to the collection of scraps that they still had, when there was a quiet metallic sound and the Hole was plunged instantly into darkness.

"Who did that?" Alex asked, hesitantly. "Geoff? Turn it on, please."

"Wasn't me," Geoff said. They could hear him flicking the switch back and forth. "Fucking thing's dead. Oh, that's just great." He breathed in, and the sound was almost a sob. "That's just fucking great. I can't see a thing."

"Nobody can," Liz said. Mike wasn't sure if he was imagining it, but he thought he could hear something like triumph in her voice.

"Has the bulb gone?" Frankie asked, sounding slightly surprised.

"Get a grip on yourself," Mike said harshly. "Of course it has."

"Oh."

"I can't believe this is happening," Alex said quietly. "It's like a nightmare that won't stop. One thing after another."

"We eat in any case," Liz said. "It's only a burned-out bulb. If that gas stove has anything left in it, we can use that for light. At least while we eat."

"OK," Geoff agreed. "I've got matches somewhere. Here."

They lit the stove, and a thin blue light washed over them. It was nearly one o'clock; they sorted out the rations. Strangely, Mike's hunger seemed to have slackened off a little. It was as Alex had said; there was still an intense burning in the pit of his stomach all the time, but he found himself increasingly able to push it to the back of his mind, make it recede from what he was thinking. It was a curious feeling: a sort of divorce of mind from body. He was pleased about it; the hunger had been very difficult to cope with.

The air in the Hole was not so good any more. The smell from the lavatory was beginning to thicken in the main room, as well.

They ate the miserable portions and drank them down with a little warm water. Mike was impressed to discover that he didn't really mind what he was given. He ate, of course, knowing that his body wouldn't keep going without it. They turned off the gas stove.

"It's dark," Frankie moaned.

"What's wrong with her?" Geoff demanded. "I don't think I can take much more of this. Of course it's dark, you stupid bitch. There isn't any light. Got it?"

"I never said I wanted to do it," Frankie cried out suddenly. "It wasn't my idea to come down here. I never said I wanted to do it. I could have been at home. I could eat whatever I wanted, do you understand?" Mike heard Liz struggle to her feet. "It wasn't my idea," Frankie shouted. "Why did you let me do this?" Her voice had risen to a hoarse scream. There was the sound of a sharp slap, and the splintering crash of glass breaking.

"Shut up," Liz said. "Calm down and behave sensibly." Another slap; then Frankie could be heard, crying softly.

"What a mess," Liz said in disgust, and her pocket flashlight snapped on, casting dim light and making the faces of those in the Hole seem to hover in midair, like masks. "That's one of the water bottles you've broken," she added. "I hope you're proud of that little stunt."

Frankie's face was white, except for a red blotch where Liz had hit her. The others stared at her, and at the broken glass and spreading water, in horror.

"Nobody *ever* hits me—" Frankie began, but before she could say another word Liz slapped her again; a hard, flat sound.

"Perhaps they should," she said. "Now sit down."

The authority in her voice was complete. Frankie hesitated, looked for a moment as if she might say something else, and then sat down abruptly. Mike stared at Liz in amazement, not knowing what had come over her. He had never seen her talk or act like this. Was she cracking up?

"I've had enough of this," she said. "I've had to hold your hands all the way through this nonsense, tell you what to do, wipe up the messes you make, tell you it's going to be all right. I'm sick of it." She turned, walked over to the water bottles and scraped the broken glass into a wet pile with her foot.

"You're like spoiled children," she said. "Can't you look after yourselves at all?"

There was an ugly silence.

"It's not that easy," Mike said. "In case you hadn't noticed, we're locked in here. I don't think we're going to get out. Martyn's not going to come, is he?"

Liz didn't even look at him.

"Of course Martyn won't let us out," she said coldly, and walked back to her sleeping bag. On the way, though, her eyes met Mike's very briefly; and in that second, he was even more astonished to see her wink at him quickly.

ELEVEN

The afternoon was worse. In the stinking darkness, Mike was aware that he frequently slipped away from the Hole, found himself more and more often wandering in a sort of dreamland, where things eventually worked out all right. Light seemed such a fundamental thing that to be without it was far worse than he could have imagined.

In the times that he was more self-aware, he worried about what Liz was doing. He couldn't make out the reason for her outburst, and he could not understand some of the things she had said. What was she up to? She had winked at him; there was a clue, there, as to what was going on, but he was unable to decipher it.

"It's dark," came Frankie's voice.

"She's crazy," Geoff said. "She's gone right over the edge. Be quiet, Frankie, can't you?"

"She's scared," Alex said. "We all are."

"I don't want to die," Frankie said.

"It'll all be OK," Alex reassured her. "Everything's going to be all right."

"Can't we stop pretending, yet?" Geoff said.

Mike was uneasy, aware that everything they said would be heard by Martyn, eventually. Was that part of what Liz was doing? And if so, why her sudden and uncharacteristic attack on them? He decided that, whatever it was, he should know; if only so that he didn't accidentally get in her way. Gradually, very slowly and quietly, he began to move over to where he knew Liz would be sitting.

"It's pointless, telling each other that it's going to be OK," Geoff went on. "We know that's not true."

"I just don't know what else to do," Alex said. "Perhaps we should pray."

"Don't make me laugh."

"Think what you like," she said. "You can't get us out of here. I can't. There's nothing we can do."

"Someone will let us out," Frankie said.

Mike felt his hand run across the edge of Liz's sleeping bag. He moved forward carefully, and touched her arm. She didn't make a sound, but almost at once he felt her move closer.

"What's happening?" he breathed, as quietly as he could.

Alex said, "I wish I could see my parents. There's so much I want to tell them, if—in case I never see them again."

"Just follow my lead," Liz whispered back. "I think this will work."

"My parents couldn't give a shit," Frankie said, and Mike was surprised to hear something of the old decisiveness back in her voice. "If they did, they would have found us and let us out. Neither of them care a damn about me."

"But they don't know where we are," Alex said. "Nobody does. I wonder if—if we could write something. In case."

"In case what?" Geoff snarled.

"Don't," Alex said quietly. "I don't feel good, Geoff. Even you should realize that. And I don't think that—I'll last too much longer. And I'm afraid. So don't."

It was Liz who spoke next. "Stop whining," she said.

"Liz—" Mike began.

"No. Don't tell me to go easy on her. She's had a few days without her normal food, for God's sake. That's all. And she thinks she's dying."

"She didn't look well at lunch," Mike said, hoping he was saying the right things.

"Neither did you," Liz said shortly. "At least you don't go on about it all the time."

"Shut up," Geoff said, nastily. "We don't have to take this from you."

"It's been a real education," Liz said. "Living down here with you guys. I'm amazed at just how easily you give up."

"There's nothing else to do," Mike shouted at her, and a little of the real despair that was still inside him must have shown through, because Liz didn't interrupt. "There's no way we can get out of here, is there? No way at all. And nobody's going to just happen to stumble on this place. It's been forgotten for years."

"Of course not," Liz said, almost pityingly. "It's the next best thing to a prison, isn't it? Oh, I give you that; Martyn's very good. Very good, indeed. But he's not perfect, not by a long way. And he made a mistake."

"What's that?" Geoff said, and he actually sounded interested.

"Not yet. First, let's pass the time by seeing why, exactly, we're here."

"I don't believe this," Alex said. "Can't you just stop going on and on about it?"

"Wait," Mike said. "I want to hear this."

"Martyn said it was an experiment with real life," Geoff said. "That was bullshit."

"How clever of you to notice," Liz said scathingly. "But have you asked yourself why, if it was so obviously bullshit, you fell for it so completely?"

"Don't talk to me like that," Geoff said. "You're here as well, remember. We all are."

"But there's a difference," Liz replied coolly. "You don't know what the hell you're doing. Mike would have flushed that cistern of water if I hadn't stopped him. Frankie threw a tantrum a while back and kicked over one of the water bottles. Alex thinks she's dying and you, Geoff—you're still trying to make yourself into something worthwhile by stamping on other people."

"You little shit," Geoff retorted savagely, and Mike heard him stand up. "You think you're so fucking cool, don't you? But you're not. You're just as fucked as the rest of us. And do you know what? I'm glad. I really am. And I'm going to keep alive long enough to hear you scream down here, to hear you come apart at the seams. Do you understand?"

"That certainly will be interesting," Liz said. "Enjoy your wait."

"Cunt," he shouted at her, and there was a scuffle in the darkness. Mike scrambled to his feet, but the place where Liz had been was empty.

Her voice, slightly breathless, came from another part of the room.

"I wouldn't slap me around too much if I were you," she said. "It wouldn't look good in the papers. Behave like a gentleman and you'll get all the credit your poor little ego needs."

"What the fuck are you talking about?" Geoff said, but he had stopped moving. Mike's heart pounded heavily in his ears.

"You're not going to *die*," Liz said scornfully. "We walk out of here at eleven o'clock tomorrow. Not that you deserve to."

"What are you talking about?" Geoff repeated, and his voice was unnaturally quiet.

"It's been like being caged up with animals," Liz said. "And just remember that you'd probably never have seen the light of day again if it wasn't for me."

"What do you mean?" It was Mike who spoke this time. "What do you mean, we're getting out tomorrow?"

"Martyn's good, but he made a bad mistake when he put me in here," Liz said. "I've—taken certain precautions. And I have him now exactly where I want him."

"Meaning?"

"It wouldn't have been enough just to escape," Liz said thoughtfully. "No. I wanted Martyn as well; I want that bastard put away for good. And so he's walking around out there, acting normally, while we're starving to death. Not a wonderful character reference, is it?"

"But no one *knows*," Mike said, in an agony of confusion.

"That's where you're wrong," Liz said. "And so is Martyn."

There was an unearthly hush.

Alex said, "Someone knows we're here? Who?"

"Do you really think I'd walk into something like this and

not be prepared?" Liz laughed. "Hardly. Yes, of course someone knows. And at eleven tomorrow, we're out of here. And
then what's Martyn going to do? It'll be our word against his,
and he won't have any excuses, any alibis, anything."

"How in heaven's name did you know this?" Mike asked,
awed by what was unfolding before him.

"I think Martyn and I are perhaps more similar than you
know," Liz said evenly. "Besides, it was obvious. I can see how
easy it must have been for him to slip up; if he thinks everyone's
as naïve as you four, then the Hole was a pretty safe bet. But like
I said, he made a mistake."

"Wait a minute," Geoff interrupted. "You're saying that
we're all right? That tomorrow we're out of here?"

"I hope I don't have to spell it out for you," Liz said.

"And you've known this all along," Geoff said slowly.

"That's a point," Mike cut in. "Why on earth didn't you
tell anyone?"

Liz sighed. "If you must know, I was quite interested to
find out how you all reacted. Not very impressive, was it?"

"That's—but that's monstrous," Mike whispered.

"Don't even try to judge me on your level," Liz snapped
back at him. "Just be grateful that you're getting out alive. You
wouldn't be, remember, if you didn't have someone to think for
you." She laughed, a low and unpleasant sound. "He's going to
be so sorry he ever tried this pitiful trick on me."

"I still can't believe it," Alex said to herself. "We're really
going to get out? It's really all right?"

"I knew it," Frankie said. "I knew we'd get out."

Liz turned on her flashlight. "So we might as well finish up this stuff," she said, sweeping the failing beam over the last scraps of food and water.

"We can eat," Mike said, incredulously. "We can really eat? Are you sure?" He looked at Liz, and the question in his eyes was far more penetrating.

"I've told you, haven't I?" she said dismissively; but before she turned away, she nodded slightly. Mike bit his lip. He thought he could see it; a huge, extremely dangerous bluff. But it had to be convincing. Hardly daring to believe what was happening, he joined the others in a riotous scramble for food and drink.

"Go easy on the water," Liz said, and for a moment Mike was terrified that she might ruin it by being too cautious. But then she added, "I want to do my teeth tomorrow morning." He smiled, and drank.

"There's still something I find hard to believe," Geoff said.

"Oh? And what might that be?"

"That you kept this quiet," he replied. "You didn't tell anyone at all. You just sat there smugly, watching us try to deal with the thought that we were going to die—and all the time you knew it was for nothing."

"You were pretty funny, sometimes," Liz said, and he hit her without warning across the face. Liz's head snapped back, and she slowly put one hand to her mouth. In the deep yellow light, the smear of blood across her cheek looked black.

"I don't give a fuck what you tell the newspapers," Geoff said, and his voice was very quiet. "You played God with us. You're no better than Martyn."

●　●　●

It hurt, of course. All of it. I knew that it was necessary, but it didn't make it any the easier. In fact, the thing I found most worrying was Mike: it was difficult for him, too, having to stand by and watch it happen. But sometimes, things have to be endured.

So at last I had put a date and a time on it. Well, we would see. Whether or not it worked was far more important than it had been before, since we now had no food and hardly any water left. All of which was a vital part of the plan, naturally; but despite my incredible hunger, that last was one of the hardest meals to finish that I have ever known. We had used up all our food, wasted water freely. It was a libation, an offering to Martyn. It had to be; it had to use up all we had left, or the bluff would not work. We had to be seen to be confident. And that was not easy for me.

Somewhere up above us, Martyn was listening. The important thing was that he would hear that conversation, hear what was effectively a challenge thrown down in front of him. Of course, if he had known that we were aware of him, he would have seen through the bluff in an instant, and just walked away. But—and this was the crux of it—if he thought that we truly believed ourselves to be isolated completely from the world outside, then there would be no reason for me to say what I had just said unless it was true. That was the key. He had to believe me. And the rest—the almost maniacal assertions that I had made—might just go home to him on an emotional level, force a response where pure reasoning could not. I was fairly sure that Martyn would bite on reasoning alone; he was far too clever to risk compromising himself when a way out was apparent. But I had to be sure.

• • •

I was sitting on the chair in his room when he came in. He was carrying a bag, a plastic bag; and it looked empty to me. I said hello. He told me it was good to see me, but he seemed preoccupied . . . nothing particularly strange, just thoughtful. He asked if I would mind waiting a while, and did I want to see him right now? I said I would like to, yes. He told me he would be just a little while, he had something to do, and he went out again. . . .

What I wanted to do was tell him that it was over, that I didn't want to see him anymore. It was going to be difficult, I knew; but I had worked it out on my own, and I thought I knew what to say and so on. I was just waiting until I had his attention, so that I could say it all properly.

He was gone over two hours. For most of that I just sat there . . . like a dog that's been told to sit. It was ridiculous, how much I'd got used to doing what he said. Eventually I got up, walked around the room. Martyn's bedroom was large enough, in a large house; but it was almost empty. There was a bed. Most boys don't make their beds, but he did—wardrobe, a desk, a chest of drawers, a rug. Nothing much else. Nothing on the walls at all. It wasn't anything like his room at school, the one full of plants and bits of pleasant clutter, the records to listen to and cushions on the floor for sitting on . . . that was the public Martyn, the one everyone knew. I don't think he liked any of that at all. He must have worked really hard to put that study together, because it can't have come naturally to him. He didn't even have a stereo in his bedroom.

In the end I thought, this is stupid . . . I can't wait here all afternoon. So I went out of the bedroom and along the corridor—I shouted out for him, but there was no reply. In the end I tried a few doors: the bathroom, one of the spare bedrooms. Maybe he'd gone out, I thought, but that seemed really strange, even if he had been carrying a bag. Then I found him. He was in a sort of lumber room further down the passage. . . . I opened the door and he was sitting there. He glanced up.

"I've been looking everywhere for you," I said. "What are you doing?"

"Nothing," he said. "Just—just listening to something."

There was a pair of headphones on the floor, and a personal stereo, and some tapes. . . . I said I wanted to talk to him, that that was why I had come in the first place. There was something wrong from that point on, as if he already knew what I was going to say. Or as if something awful had happened. . . . I don't know. But all of a sudden I was scared—scared of him.

He looked at me, and said, "Right, let's talk." Just like that, as if he hadn't vanished for two hours.

We went back to his bedroom and I sat down. He was walking up and down, rubbing his hands together. I remember thinking he looked sort of funny, doing that. . . . I started on what I wanted to tell him, about how I really liked him, but that I didn't think our relationship was going anywhere . . . meaningless stuff, but everybody knows what it means. I knew he wasn't listening after a bit. His mind was somewhere else completely.

I got up and stood in front of him. "I'm trying to talk to you," I said. He just looked at me, like he'd never seen me before, but I plunged on. I said, "I don't think this is working out," and tried to get him to understand.

He took hold of my shoulders and said, "Don't you love me?"

It was so strange—I said, "Of course I like you, but I just think that maybe we'd be happier if we spent some time on our own."

There was a weird look in his eyes. . . . I remember he said, "Do you want to get away from me, then?"

And I said, "It might be best . . . for a while. . . ."

And then—then he was holding me tightly, so tight that it hurt; I was about to say something, to tell him to stop, but I looked into his face and I thought that if I spoke he'd kill me . . . it was that strong, and so sudden and awful that I didn't know what to do. I think I must have cried out because he told me to be quiet. And then he said—he was talking, about . . . he said the most terrible things—on and on. It was like listening to a nightmare talking—and I can hardly remember a word, because I really believed he would kill me. I don't know why. I knew it. . . .

He—and then—

I stopped the tape. What had happened to this girl was my fault, in a way; it was my action from within the Hole that had affected Martyn, which had impacted so forcibly on his constructed personality that for a while it had been weakened, and some of what lay underneath had shown through. Lisa was the only person to see the true face of Martyn. I shuddered, picked up the pen and let the recording continue.

He pushed me down, and I fell . . . not onto the bed, onto the floor, and it hurt like crazy, and he—said, then, that he loved me, but he was laughing and—he held me down, there wasn't anything I could do. I said—I shouted at him to stop, and tried to scream, and he—he just . . . he just put his hand into my mouth, so I couldn't make any sound—just put his hand in, as if that was all it took to keep me quiet . . . and—and he pulled down my pants, with his other hand. I bit him, then, because finally I knew that this was really happening, and it was so stupid because I bit and bit on his fingers, and there was blood everywhere and in my mouth and Christ I swallowed it but he never even flinched—it was like he couldn't feel a thing, nothing at all . . . and—he just held me down and—and he just pushed himself inside me, and I tried to stop him but there was nothing I could do . . . it was like being torn open, inside, and I had his blood on my face and in my eyes, but I could still see him. . . .

And then he stopped, and got off me, still with his hand there so that I couldn't talk. I was choking and gagging, and he told me then . . . he said that if I—if I told anyone, no matter where I was, he would find me . . . and I believed him. He meant it . . . I could see in his eyes that he meant it. I've never been so terrified. . . .

And it was so senseless. At the time there was just the pain, and the—and shock, I suppose, I don't know . . . but it was senseless. He was only—he only did it for a short time. I don't think he even—he didn't even come, didn't even get any pleasure out of—doing it, I think. So what was the point? Christ, why did he do it to me? It was as if he was—punishing me, for something I hadn't done, didn't know I'd done, anyway.

And again, listening to her voice, I can't keep from crying.

When night came, those in the Hole settled down to sleep relatively easily for the first time in several days.

"Eleven o'clock tomorrow," Frankie said happily. "That's only fourteen hours away."

"Go to sleep and it'll come all the sooner," Alex said. She still sounded sick, Mike noticed; but she no longer sounded despairing. That was the difference, ironically: that he and Liz, who before had been the only ones with any reason for hope, were now the ones who felt least secure, knowing that their survival pivoted on a bluff that might or might not work.

Gradually, they tailed off into sleep. Mike lay staring at the ceiling, waiting impatiently until everyone was settled. Allowing a safe margin, he crept out of his sleeping bag and went through to the second room, holding his breath as he passed the lavatory. A minute or two later Liz joined him.

"You were fantastic," he whispered. "It'll work. It has to."

"Thanks. We'll soon see, won't we? It all depends on Martyn. I think he'll fall for it. He's too confident; he won't imagine that we've found a way out from in here, so he'll be left having to believe that I'm telling the truth."

"The others hate you," Mike said.

"It's only for another few hours, like Frankie said. I can put up with that." She hesitated. "Mike?"

"Yes?"

"Do you really think we'll get out?"

"Really, yes. You were brilliant."

"Geoff was brilliant," she said.

"He hurt you. I didn't know what to do."

"Doing nothing was right," she said. "You're supposed to hate me just as much as the others."

"And you think Martyn will buy this?"

"I think so. Being criticized was important, because I had to end up sounding—well, as much like him as possible, in a way. And I insulted his pride. He won't let me get away with that." She paused. "Mike? Do you really think it'll work? Truly?"

"I hope so. Yes. Yes, you did it."

"We did it," she corrected. "And there's not so long to wait, now. Tomorrow I'll be able to do all the things I normally do. I can walk and breathe clean air, and see colors. I could build as many bloody sheds as I like."

Mike laughed quietly. "And I shall eat and eat and eat," he said, feeling a silly excitement tingling inside him. "I shall order mountains of food."

"And we can revise," Liz giggled.

"Seriously. We can tell everyone about Martyn," Mike said.

"Ah," Liz said, after a moment. "That. Wait and see, Mike."

"Why?"

"Because he'll have a good excuse, never fear. He'll be here in good time, well before eleven, and he'll let us out and everything will just be a big mistake. Mark my words, he'll get away with it."

"He will *not*," Mike said hotly.

"We'll see. But I think that the price we pay for getting out is to grant Martyn immunity. I don't think we can avoid that."

"That's crazy," Mike protested. "He can't just get away with it."

"He's too clever," Liz said. "Far too clever. He'll find a way, just as we did."

"There has to be something we can do——" Mike began.

"Shh." He heard her shuffle across the floor until she was next to him. "Hold me."

Gently, he put his arm around her shoulders.

"I really like you," she said quietly. "I'm glad you were here. I don't know ... maybe I would never have thought of it all without you."

"Don't be silly," he said. "It was brilliant."

"I think it *will* work," she said. "I really do. I think tomorrow we'll be out of this——nightmare." She laughed suddenly, crazily.

"What is it?"

"I was——sorry. I was going to say would you like to come to tea sometime? And then I realized what it would sound like."

Slowly, Mike began to laugh, too, until they were both rocking helplessly with silent mirth, trying to keep quiet.

"Anyway——" Liz spluttered. "Hang on. Anyway, what I wanted to say wasn't that. It's just that——I think we're OK, I really do. But we might not be. He might not fall for it. So—— let's just make the most of what we've got now, all right? Just in case."

Mike stroked her hair back from her face. "OK," he whispered. And then, "I love you. I really think I do."

Liz sighed; and they held each other in silence for a long time. At last, clumsily, they helped each other off with their clothes and spread them out on the stone floor. Lying huddled in the rank darkness, they touched, and kissed; stroked each other and shivered together. Mike pulled her beneath him, and they clung tightly. Their lovemaking was awkward, uncomfortable to begin with; but somewhere they found how to make it good, and at the end the darkness was lifted briefly.

TWELVE

They slept where they were, and for once Mike's sleep was peaceful. When morning came, they crept back to their places in the main room. Although they hadn't spoken, Mike knew what must have been going through Liz's mind: that they no longer had any food or water at all, and that if Martyn did not come, they would have speeded up their own deaths. The minutes began cranking past with unbearable slowness.

The others, unaware of what was actually confronting them, were noisily exuberant; Frankie had lit the gas stove once more and was trying to brush her hair, holding a pocket mirror in one hand.

"I look a disgrace," she pronounced. "Do you really think we'll be in the papers?"

"I should think so," Geoff said.

"Do you realize what a scandal it will be?" Mike said, trying to join in. "Everybody's always thought that Martyn was so fantastic. Think what's going to happen now."

"Not everybody," Liz reminded him.

"I should keep quiet, if I were you," Geoff said. "We haven't forgotten what you did."

"I don't understand you, Liz," Alex said. "I thought you were—you were always so friendly."

"Look, I didn't want anyone dead, that's all," Liz said. "But don't try and pretend we were friends. Don't try to make out that you were best buddies with me. Go glory-hunting somewhere else."

"I wouldn't be called your friend for a million pounds," Geoff said.

"What time is it?" Frankie asked.

"You really are back to normal," Mike observed.

"We're getting out," Frankie said. "I still can't get over it."

"It's about half past eight," Geoff told her. "A while to go, yet."

"What's everyone going to do?" Alex asked. "First thing you're going to do?"

"Have a bath," Mike said. "I stink. So do the rest of you, if you don't mind my saying so."

They laughed. "I feel terrible," Geoff said. "I want to get clean, and then do something active. I've been sitting on my arse for—how many days has it been? Anyway, too long. Go for a run, or something."

"You're welcome," Frankie said. "Don't expect me to join you, though."

Mike listened to the conversation, incredulous. It was as if nothing at all had happened; they were talking, and laughing, just as they had the first night. The days in between didn't seem to have impinged on them. He shook his head, and winced; there was a headache starting high up in there. It was almost farcical that only a matter of hours ago, these people had been expecting to die—even waiting for it, and now this expectation had been washed away without a trace.

He recognized why he was thinking like this. No matter what the others were saying about Liz now, they trusted her. They might hate her, but without realizing it they were still taking her word in complete faith. The other three had no doubts that they would be free soon, while Mike had far too many.

Was this really going to be the end of it all? Despite what Liz had said the night before, Mike was still determined that Martyn would pay for what he had done. There had to be a way. And there was more: last night he had slept with a girl whom he had come to depend on. He had said, back then, that he loved her; and now, when it was becoming possible that he could walk away from her for good, he found that he actually did. He glanced across to Liz, with this thought running through his mind, and saw her smile at him quickly.

"Who is this friend of yours, then?" Frankie asked Liz. "The one that's coming to let us out."

"You won't know her," Liz said.

I put down the pen and cupped my face in my hands. Looking out there, across the trees, the roofs of Our Glorious School, I could see the sun shining on the weather vanes and lightning rods that bristle on the gray slate. Someone in a red tracksuit was running through the woods, I saw; and in the tangle of our garden, below, there were rainbows shimmering in the water from the sprinklers. The varnish on my desk was glowing the color of honey.

There was a curious feeling inside me. I pulled on a pair of sneakers and went downstairs, through the empty hall and out of our huge chocolate-colored front door. The driveway was sprouting weeds again; I hadn't been seeing to things the way I normally did, and it showed. I made off towards the village, keeping to the road. Twice, there are bridges where the river cuts across and back; and at each I stopped, looked down into the tumbling water. When I was small, there had been boats to sail down the river, made out of wood scraps from my father's shed. A very long time ago; all that was long gone now, left behind. You could drop the boat in at one road bridge, and then run along to the next as fast as you could. Sometimes the boat would come through, circling proudly as you cheered it on, and then make off in halts and surges towards—where? The sea, I always thought. Perhaps some of them even reached the sea.

The village was slow in the heat of the afternoon. I went through the market square to the back streets, past the Horseman and up the low hill on the other side. I wasn't going anywhere, not really; just walking. The story was nearly finished, but it wasn't just that. I didn't want to write an ending so soon.

At nine o'clock, they heard a sound outside the door.

"Hey!" Frankie shouted. "We're in here!"

There was a clamor; shouting and shrieks as they heard the padlock being slowly undone.

"Be careful," Liz shouted. "There's a drop on this side." Mike was impressed; even at the last, she kept up the charade.

The door faltered, seemed stuck for a moment. Then it was heaved open, and in the unbearably bright light that poured down onto them, they glimpsed a figure in the doorway.

Mike, blinded and unable to see a thing, nevertheless heard Liz very clearly; "What the *fuck*?"

"Hi there!" Frankie was shouting. "You're early. Have you brought a ladder or something?"

"I can't believe we're finally out of here," Alex said. "Oh, thank God we are."

Liz's voice cut across them all. "Who is that?" she shouted. "Who's there?"

There was a pause, and the shouting died down as the others began to realize what she had said. Eyes turned to Liz, whose face was as bright as flame in the light from the doorway.

"Who *are* you?" she said, more quietly.

The figure above them crouched down by the door.

"Liz? Is that you? Oh God," it said. "This is—oh dear God, what do I do?"

"Lisa?" The expression of sheer surprise on Liz's face was almost comic. "You have to get us out. Quickly, before Martyn gets here."

"Martyn's gone," Lisa said. "How long have you—no, wait. How do I get you out?"

"A ladder," Liz shouted back. "Hurry."

"OK. I'll be as quick as I can." She turned, and slipped away into the brightness above them.

"What's going on?" Mike asked, breathless. "That wasn't Martyn."

"Of course it wasn't," Frankie said, puzzled. "But I thought we didn't know this friend of yours? Everyone knows Lisa."

"Shut up," Mike said. "None of you know—anything. Liz?"

"I don't understand," she said. "What does she mean, Martyn's gone? Nothing makes sense."

"What are you two talking about?" Geoff asked. "I thought you knew about all this."

"It's too complicated to explain now," Liz said. "But—she shouldn't be here. What's happening?"

After a while, they heard a sharp crash and the ringing of struck metal from nearby. A few seconds later Lisa struggled into view with a wooden ladder. "I dropped it down the stairs," she said. "My God, how long have you been down here? You look like ghosts."

"Please hurry," Alex said.

"OK. Here—try and catch the end before it falls over."

She slid the ladder down the wall of the Hole, where it was grasped at once by eager hands.

"There," she called down to them. "Is that all right?"

"Fine," Liz said. "Come on, you guys. Up you go."

Mike hung back. "Liz? This wasn't part of the plan, was it?"

She shook her head. "Not to my knowledge. But at least we're out. Be thankful for small mercies." And then, with a sudden grin, she threw her arms around him and hugged him. "Come on. Let's get out of here."

They hurried up, leaving the Hole behind, and into the sunlight.

Five days later, I took a walk in the woods at dusk. A lot had been pieced together by that time; a lot had become clear. Martyn had gone, and nobody knew where. The bluff had worked, in so far that we had escaped, but the method of our escape was not one that I had foreseen. Lisa, of course; and by the time we were released, Martyn was already twelve hours distant in some unknown direction.

So I believed.

Lisa, alone in his house, had put together some of the things he had said before he left, and come up with a horrific and incredible story which she was almost unable to believe. But the cassettes which Martyn left behind were enough, in the end: they were from early on, and she caught the reference to the English block quickly enough. The tapes that might have—that could have proved something—had all gone.

Outwardly, at that time, I didn't look bad. The cut on my face where Geoff had hit me was almost unnoticeable, and I felt a lot better. It was surprising how little we had deteriorated, in those days in the Hole; physically, at least. We were dirty, sure—and thinner, of course. But after a wash, there was nothing too strikingly different. We were young and resilient, I suppose. But the scars that take time to heal are those inside.

As to where Martyn is *now*, I truly do not know. But that evening, in the woods, I made myself a promise: to keep alert, to keep awake. Not for my own protection, because Martyn has done with me, I think. But when one day he reappears, some time far away in the future, at least one person will be forewarned.

"That's it," I say, putting down the stack of paper.

"That's really it."

"Finished?"

"Yes."

"And you told everything?"

I smile. "No. But there's enough in there."

"That's good."

"I've got a question for you."

"Really? What might that be?"

"A long time ago—I don't know if you remember this."

"Try me," he says.

"A long time ago, I asked you what you wished, and you said you'd tell me, once the writing was over."

"I did?"

"Yes," I say. "Tease. You do remember."

"Oh! That. Well, maybe."

"So?"

"So what?"

I smile. "Don't mess me around. What was the wish, then?"

"Ah." He looks out of the window. "You see out there?"

"Yes."

"There's still enough light to get to the village. We could have a drink."

"Sounds good. Tell me on the way, then."

"Right."

We walk out of the attic together, close the door behind us.

EPILOGUE

SOME PRELIMINARY OBSERVATIONS ON
THE HOLE

That, then, is *The Hole*—an intense narrative that Elizabeth achieved in four months. Coming, as it did, after a protracted period of almost total silence, it was a considerable shock, not least because it revealed the workings of an incisive and imaginative intellect. Elizabeth's school reports from the time immediately preceding the Hole provide a fair general understanding of her capabilities, and, if anything, *The Hole* exceeds what might be expected of her. Since it was the opinion of many investigators at the time of the incident that Elizabeth's trauma-induced withdrawal might be permanent—that she might never regain access to the parts of her mind inside the barriers that she slammed up—*The Hole* represents not only the most important development for Elizabeth for the past six years, but also one of the most exciting documents of recent psychoanalytical history.

The text itself purports to tell the story of the Hole. In as much as the Hole existed, and Elizabeth and four others experienced it, her account is accurate. Indeed, her accuracy goes beyond this overview to the extent that the early parts of Elizabeth's account correspond extremely closely to the chain of events outlined by Dr. E. Lawrence immediately following the incident (see "The Structure and Effects of Social Deprivation: recent case histories," by Eliot Lawrence). Thereafter, however, Elizabeth's distinctions between objective reality and subjective fantasy become increasingly confused, although the internal consistency of *The Hole* narrative is sustained throughout with remarkably few errors (rather, the subjective illusion is integrated into the narrative almost seamlessly: notable oversights and/or possibly intentional slips will be discussed below). As far as can be reasonably assessed, passages set *in* the Hole are largely accurate and correspond to Dr. Lawrence's account up to chapter eight of the text. (An interesting point is that Elizabeth uses the omniscient viewpoint prevalent in contemporary literature for the passages dealing with events *in* the Hole, but switches to a personal, first-person viewpoint for the remaining portions of the story. The intention, it seems clear, is to help her create an artificial distance between herself and the memories evoked by the narrative in those situations where the narrative necessarily deals with trauma. This technique appears to be a limited success: up to chapter eight—and for some portions of the text thereafter—events within the Hole as described by Elizabeth fit Dr. Lawrence's chronology closely. That is, by creating such an artificial boundary, Elizabeth allows herself the freedom to describe events which actually affected *her*, but without having to participate actively in their reconstruction during the writing of the text.)

After chapter eight, however, it can be seen that Elizabeth relies more and more on her "alternative ending," wherein she deftly manipulates the situation in the Hole in such a way that the entire group survives. It is important to realize that the ramifications of this alternative were evidently deeply entrenched even as Elizabeth embarked on the narrative, since she postulates a long-term relationship with "Mike" outside the Hole from the very beginning of the text. Apart from one or two occasions when she lets slip that there is in fact a far greater span of elapsed time between the occasion of the Hole and the writing of the story than she would have the reader believe, the illusion is extremely successful, and reads convincingly. (It is generally accepted that Michael Rollins died on the sixteenth day.)

In keeping with her school education, Elizabeth sees fit to add to the basic text some quite ambitious layers of metaphor and symbolism. For the most part, this is handled with a remarkable maturity. Most clumsy and obvious is the "dream summer" device which she employs, in which events outside the Hole occur. There is a moment of confusion in her concluding paragraphs when bright light streams into the Hole from the open doorway. (She has already stated quite plainly that the door to the Hole, being along a short passage, is out of direct sunlight.) The "dream summer" serves, if anything, as a calming influence, to stabilize and balance the increasingly frequent moments of emotional distress which the narrative must have caused her. The subjective comfort of the constructed fantasy offers a retreat from her reaction to the recollected nature of the Hole.

Apart from this, there are the darker aspects of the Hole narrative itself to be considered. The alternative version Elizabeth portrays is not entirely idyllic. It becomes inceasingly clear that the character of "Lisa" is central to a comprehensive understanding of the text. Elizabeth sketches Lisa only briefly, and references made to her are erratic. This, in itself, is enough to distinguish Lisa from the other characters of *The Hole*. The peculiar mechanism that Elizabeth utilizes to present Lisa's contributions to the text—through tape recordings—is significant, in that it allows Lisa's monologues to approach a stream-of-consciousness quality. When the structure of these passages is compared to the remainder of the text, it quickly becomes apparent that, while elsewhere Elizabeth has imposed her own concepts of style and form on her writing, the "Lisa" passages are far less organized. Also significant is the similarity between the names of the two characters in the text, where Elizabeth refers to herself exclusively as "Liz." It seems almost certain that the two characters are, in fact, dissembled personas constituting the whole character of Elizabeth herself. (There is no evidence to support a belief that "Lisa" ever actually existed.) At first it would seem strange that Elizabeth chooses to split her textual character in two like this, but she does it with, it appears, good reason. If it is assumed that the two are, in essence, the same person, then several points previously unimportant become more relevant. Firstly, it becomes apparent that Elizabeth knew "Martyn," perhaps intimately, *before* the Hole. The maneuver Elizabeth perfoms, of telling a part of her own story as if from the point of view of someone else, is an important distancing device. Like the continual swapping of narrative perspective mentioned earlier, it enables her to include in her story events which she is not yet prepared to link actively to herself. (It is interesting to note, with reference to Elizabeth's handwritten manuscript, that while she works and reworks most sections of the text—frequently achieving a higher degree of objectivity as a result—the "Lisa" passages are without exception left exactly as written. The quality of handwriting deteriorates, and the incidence of spelling mistakes increases—especially Elizabeth's habitual quirk of adding the letter *s* indiscriminately to word endings—as if many of the conscious critical faculties have been suspended. It is probable that there is a large degree of catharsis associated with these passages, and Elizabeth has avoided revising them in order to avoid having to read, and thereby experience, the events they relate a second time.)

Another, more disturbing implication arising from the Liz/Lisa association also comes to light. It is first important to recognize what kind of a person Elizabeth portrays herself as in the course of the text. She repeatedly personifies herself as being tough, independent, self-willed; as being able to cope with situations on a number of levels, and as being a leader of others. There is little reason to doubt this assessment of her personality; it is consistent with the school's impression of her, and consistent with the life she led at home, caring on her own for a crippled mother. But her self-reliance in the Hole can, at times, seem contrived. (Her idealization of herself does not stop at a mental level; rather whimsically, she describes herself in the text as being of slight physical build, with "small hands.") It is a measure of her own intellect and determination that Elizabeth wrote such a convincing alternative ending. The reality of the Hole, of course, was very different. And here, any analysis of the text must arrive at a highly significant point. In the text there is an extremely close proximity between Liz's account of her lovemaking with Mike, and Lisa's account of her rape. If the two characters are indeed linked, as most observers agree, then the suggestion is plainly that, whatever sexual encounter *did* occur in the Hole, Elizabeth may not have participated in it as freely as she would have the reader imagine. It seems likely that the event is confused in her own mind to the extent that it, too, splits in half: half idealized, romantic sex, and half painful and violent violation.

That Elizabeth blames herself, at least in part, for the outcome of the Hole would be easier to understand if she had, as previously discussed, known "Martyn" beforehand. If she felt in any way that she should have been able to see what was going to happen, before it was too late, then the burden of guilt—however wrongly placed it may seem from the outside—would naturally be greatly increased. Strangely, Elizabeth's descriptions of "Martyn" bring the reader no closer to ascertaining who he or she was. The actual existence of "Martyn" as a physical person has been called into question, although there is strong evidence in the text to indicate that "Martyn" is *not* a fictitious creation. Elizabeth makes a point several times of linking "Martyn" with documented events outside the Hole (most notably "the Gibbon incident"; the text picks up events some six months after Major Gibson's retirement). From Elizabeth's account it would appear obvious that "Martyn" pursued an autonomous existence within the school community; the lack of corroborative testimony from those in her year group, and the intentional misdirection involved in portraying "Martyn" as the master-mind of a series of easily attributable pranks, serves only to underline the fact that Elizabeth treats "Martyn" in a deliberately evasive manner. It would seem obvious, one might imagine, that to reveal the identity of "Martyn" would be to absolve Elizabeth as the only survivor of the Hole. Evidently, Elizabeth does not think so.

A more comprehensive and exhaustive analysis of the text will follow shortly.

Dear Eliot—

It's certainly my hope that this marks the beginning of Elizabeth's emergence from a world of silence. That the story is the result of her own decision is, I'm sure you'll agree, extremely encouraging, as is the large degree of accurate content . . . and the portions of the work which don't yet represent the actuality of the Hole are certainly a first step in coming to terms with that actuality, and dealing with it. There's a long way to go, but I think that eventually we'll be able to give Elizabeth her life back. I have not yet felt in me that the Hole is finished.

Dr. Philippa Horwood